CW01499684

URBAN
LEGENDS
from
UK

F.T. Weaver

West Agora Int

Timisoara 2025

WEST AGORA INT S.R.L.

West Agora Int

F.T. Weaver

Urban Legends from UK

Volume 1

Chilling Tales from British Towns and Countryside

Urban Legends from UK Copyright © 2025 West Agora Int
westagoraint@gmail.com

Published by West Agora Int
Edited by West Agora Int
Cover Art by West Agora Int

Dare You Peer into Britain's Shadowed Heart?

Beyond the postcard vistas and bustling city streets of the United Kingdom lies another Britain – a land steeped in mist and mystery, where ancient fears whisper on the wind and the inexplicable lurks just beyond the veil of the ordinary. Within these pages, F.T. Weaver, your personal guide to the uncanny, flings open the creaking doors to this hidden realm, inviting you to explore ten of its most chilling and enduring urban legends.

Prepare to feel the icy breath of a **fiery-eyed phantom** leaping across Victorian London rooftops, and listen for the mournful howl of **Black Shuck**, the spectral hound whose appearance across East Anglian fens is a harbinger of doom. Journey to Cornwall, where a **phantom panther** is said to stalk the shadowed expanse of Bodmin Moor, and venture into a North London cemetery where a **king vampire** reputedly held sway, sparking a modern-day panic.

Will you offer a ride to the **sorrowful spirit** who haunts the lonely bends of Blue Bell Hill, forever seeking a destination she'll never reach? Can you brave the ancient halls of Hampton Court Palace, where the **Grey Lady** glides, her sorrow an almost tangible presence? Steel yourself against the terror that gripped an ordinary Enfield home, besieged by an **unseen tormentor** whose disembodied voice chilled a nation.

Then, gaze into the **abyssal, peat-stained depths** of Loch Ness, pondering the ancient mystery that may, or may not, reside there. Confront the **cursed relic** in a remote Dorset manor, a screaming skull that refuses to be silenced, its rage echoing through centuries. And finally, marvel at the medieval enigma of the **otherworldly children with skin of green**, who emerged from the very earth of Suffolk, their origins a question that still baffles and beguiles.

These are more than mere tales; they are the resonant echoes of deep-seated anxieties, the unexplained phenomena that cling to specific places, and the haunting mysteries that refuse to be forgotten. Retold with a chilling new potency, these legends will draw you into the very heart of Britain's hidden fears.

Turn the page, if you dare. The shadows are waiting.

Dedication

For the ancient stones and shadowed lanes of the British Isles,
whose echoes hold the whispers of these unsettling tales.
And for every listener, past and present,
who has felt the thrill of a story told in the dimming light,
and dared to wonder what truly lurks just beyond the fire's
glow.
May these legends find you, and may you find a piece of their
enduring mystery within.

– F.T. Weaver

TABLE OF CONTENTS

Spring-Heeled Jack

The year was 1837. Gas lamps, a relatively new marvel, cast pools of hesitant light upon London's cobbled streets, but beyond their reach, shadows clung thick and heavy, gravid with the unsaid and the unseen. Queen Victoria had only just ascended the throne, and an air of bustling progress warred with an older, deeper sense of unease. The city was a labyrinth of stark contrasts: grand townhouses standing aloof from sprawling, lightless slums; the clatter of commerce barely drowning out the whispers from forgotten alleyways. And it was from these liminal spaces, these fringes where the known world frayed into uncertainty, that the first tendrils of a peculiar dread began to creep.

Initial reports were vague, dismissed by most as the imaginings of overwrought minds or the product of too much gin. A lone woman hurrying home through the twilight lanes of Barnes Common spoke of a tall, cloaked figure that seemed to melt from the mist, only to vanish with an impossible leap over a high wall when she cried out. A lamplighter in a dimly lit suburb swore he saw eyes glowing from the dark recesses of a churchyard, eyes that belonged to something that moved with an unnatural, bounding gait. These were isolated incidents, pebbles dropped into the vast pond of London life, their ripples quickly fading. They were curiosities, quickly forgotten by a city preoccupied with its own relentless momentum.

But the whispers persisted, like the damp chill that seeped from the Thames. They spoke of a "ghost," a "devil," or some monstrous "bear" or "ape" that stalked the night. These were the usual phantoms conjured by nervous communities, yet there was a nuance here, a thread of something more tangibly malevolent.

Then came the account of Mary Stevens.

It was a cool October evening. Mary, a servant girl, was making her way towards Lavender Hill, near Clapham Common, after visiting her parents in Battersea. The path was familiar, yet the encroaching darkness felt different that night, heavier somehow, the silence punctuated only by the distant rumble of carriages and her own quickening footsteps. As she passed a particularly shadowed alleyway, a figure detached itself from the blackness with startling speed. He was tall, Mary would later recount, his form obscured by a dark cloak, but it was his grip that seared itself into her memory.

Before she could scream, he seized her arms, his fingers described as cold, vice-like, and disturbingly strong. She felt not flesh, but something harder, something that scraped against her skin – like claws, she stammered to the disbelieving constables.

He did not speak, but instead, pressed his face close to hers. What she saw in the gloom would fuel her nightmares for years: eyes that seemed to glow with a reddish intensity, like hot coals. His breath was foul, and a low, guttural sound emanated from him. Then, in a horrifying display of violation, he began to kiss her face, his lips icy, while his metallic-feeling claws ripped at her clothes and tore at her skin.

Mary's terror finally found its voice in a series of piercing shrieks. The sudden, desperate sound seemed to startle her assailant. He released her abruptly and, with a single, astonishing bound, cleared a high fence that bordered the path, disappearing into the gloom of a nearby garden as if swallowed by the night itself. Neighbours, alerted by her screams, found her collapsed and hysterical, her clothes torn, her body trembling.

The account was met with skepticism by the authorities, who were inclined to believe it the work of a common ruffian, perhaps embellished by a frightened young woman. But Mary Stevens was adamant. This was no ordinary man. The glowing eyes, the claw-like hands, and above all, that impossible leap – these were details that would soon weave themselves into the terrifying tapestry of a legend, a legend that was just beginning to stitch itself into the very fabric of London's darkest fears. The name was not yet known, but the entity that would become Spring-Heeled Jack had made his first truly chilling mark.

The Mary Stevens incident, though disturbing, might have faded into the annals of London's countless unsolved assaults had it remained isolated. But it was not to be. As the autumn of 1837 bled into a grim winter, the nebulous terror that had haunted the city's periphery began to coalesce, taking on a more defined and infinitely more frightful form. The phantom of

Barnes Common and Lavender Hill was about to earn his infamous moniker.

Several months after Mary Stevens' ordeal, reports of a similar figure harassing women began to surface with alarming frequency. Then, on a cold February night in 1838, came the attack that would truly ignite public panic and sear the image of this agile menace into the Victorian consciousness. Lucy Scales, a young woman of eighteen, was walking home with her sister through a respectable area near Green Dragon Alley in Limehouse. The narrow passage was ill-lit, the kind of place where shadows played tricks on the eyes. As they hurried along, a tall, cloaked figure suddenly emerged from the darkness.

Before Lucy could react, the figure spat a torrent of what she described as blue and white flames directly into her face. The searing heat, the terrifying, unnatural colour of the fire, sent a shockwave of agony and terror through her. She collapsed to the ground, temporarily blinded and overcome by violent fits. Her sister's screams and the commotion drew others to the scene, but the attacker had vanished as quickly as he had appeared, leaping away with incredible bounds. Lucy Scales was left profoundly shaken, her vision impaired for some time, the ghastly image of those spectral flames forever imprinted on her mind.

Just days later, the entity struck again, this time with an encounter that would provide the most detailed and chilling description yet. Jane Alsop, living in Bearbind Lane, Old Ford, heard a violent knocking at her front door late one evening. A voice from outside, claiming to be a policeman, shouted, "For God's sake, bring me a light, for we have caught Spring-heeled Jack here in the lane!"

Relieved that the mysterious tormentor might finally be

apprehended, Jane rushed to the door with a candle. As she opened it, she found not a policeman, but a figure of nightmarish aspect. He wore a kind of helmet and a tight-fitting white garment that appeared like an oilskin, shimmering strangely in the candlelight. His eyes, she would later insist, were like red balls of fire. Instead of a lantern, he held what looked like a small lamp, from which he could apparently direct the blasts of blue flame that had so terrified Lucy Scales.

Before Jane could retreat, he lunged, seizing her by the neck and shoulders. His hands, she recounted with horror, were not human; they were cold and clammy as a corpse's, and at their tips were sharp, metallic claws that tore through her dress and cruelly raked her flesh. He began to drag her towards the gate, his grip like iron. Jane's screams, however, alerted her sisters. As they rushed to her aid, the attacker, perhaps unnerved by their numbers or simply having achieved his sadistic purpose, let her go. He didn't just run; he bounded away, clearing the high gate with ease and disappearing into the night, his laughter, a hideous, ringing sound, echoing behind him.

The Alsop attack, vividly reported in the newspapers, particularly The Times, caused a sensation. The details were so specific, so grotesque: the glowing eyes, the tight, shimmering costume, the metallic claws, the terrifying leaps, and the ability to spew fire. It was this last ability, coupled with his astonishing agility, that solidified his name in the public lexicon. He was no mere ghost or common ruffian. He was "Spring-Heeled Jack," a name that resonated with both his incredible jumping prowess and the sudden, spring-like manner of his attacks.

London was now firmly in the grip of fear. Women hesitated to venture out after dark. Men armed themselves, forming impromptu patrols. The previously scattered whispers had become a roar of collective anxiety. Spring-Heeled Jack was no longer a rumour confined to the shadowy outskirts; he was a tangible threat, a fiery demon who could appear anywhere, attack without warning, and vanish without a trace, leaving only terror and bewildered outrage in his wake. The hunt was truly on, but the hunter seemed to possess abilities that defied all rational explanation.

The vivid, chilling details of the Alsop attack, splashed across the pages of London's newspapers, transformed Spring-Heeled Jack from a localized menace into a city-wide, even national, obsession. The fear was palpable, a living entity that stalked the streets alongside the mysterious figure himself. It seeped into homes, darkened conversations, and made every unexpected noise in the night a potential harbinger of unimaginable terror. The name "Spring-Heeled Jack" was on everyone's lips, whispered with a mixture of dread and morbid fascination.

The sheer public outcry could no longer be ignored by the authorities. Sir John Cowan, the Lord Mayor of London, found himself compelled to address the issue publicly at the Mansion House. He revealed a letter he had received some weeks prior, penned by a "resident of Peckham," detailing several instances where young women in the area had been accosted by a figure matching Jack's description. The letter spoke of a "wager by some profligate young men of rank," suggesting that the culprit was a reckless nobleman engaging in a cruel and dangerous prank, using a cleverly disguised costume and perhaps some theatrical contraption to achieve his terrifying leaps and fiery breath. The Lord Mayor, while acknowledging the widespread alarm, expressed his skepticism about the more fantastical elements but promised that measures were being taken. Police officers were deployed in greater numbers, particularly in the areas of reported attacks, and plainclothes detectives mingled with the populace, hoping to ensnare the elusive phantom.

This official acknowledgment, however, did little to quell the hysteria; if anything, it validated the public's fear. If the Lord Mayor himself was discussing Spring-Heeled Jack, then the threat was undeniably real. Vigilante groups began to form. Men, armed with pistols, cudgels, and whatever makeshift weapons they could find, patrolled their neighborhoods, determined to protect their families and unmask the villain. The atmosphere was thick with suspicion. Any tall, cloaked individual behaving erratically, any sudden unexplained noise, could trigger a panicked chase or an angry mob. More than one innocent eccentric found themselves unpleasantly accosted by these self-appointed guardians of the peace.

Spring-Heeled Jack, however, remained infuriatingly elusive, almost as if he reveled in the chaos he created. He seemed to taunt his pursuers. There were reports of him being cornered, only to execute one of his astounding leaps over a high wall or onto a rooftop, his mocking laughter drifting back to the frustrated crowd below. He was seen, or claimed to be seen, in various guises – sometimes in his tight-fitting oilskins and helmet, sometimes in more gentlemanly attire, but always with those unsettling, glowing eyes and that terrifying agility.

The theories about his identity swirled like the London fog. Was he indeed a deranged nobleman, perhaps the "Mad Marquess" of Waterford, known for his reckless behavior and cruel practical jokes? Or was he an escaped lunatic with uncanny physical prowess? Some whispered of a foreign acrobat or a disgruntled inventor putting some infernal device to nefarious use. Others, particularly those who had allegedly witnessed his more supernatural feats, clung to darker explanations: he was a demon escaped from the pits of Hell, a spectral visitant, or some unholy hybrid of man and beast. The lack of any discernible motive for his attacks – which seemed designed purely to terrify rather than to rob or inflict lasting physical harm beyond the initial assault – only deepened the mystery and fueled the more outlandish speculations.

And then, the sightings began to spread beyond the confines of London. Like a malevolent spore carried on the wind, tales of Spring-Heeled Jack, or figures remarkably similar, started to emerge from other parts of the country. He was reportedly seen in Lincolnshire, his leaps clearing five-barred gates with ease. Accounts from the Midlands described a figure breathing blue flames and terrorizing villagers. Each new report added another layer to the legend, transforming him from a specific London menace into a nationwide bogeyman, a protean figure of fear who could manifest anywhere, anytime. The hunt for Spring-Heeled Jack had become a desperate, sprawling affair, but the quarry remained always one impossible leap ahead, a phantom dancing just beyond the reach of comprehension and capture.

As the years turned into decades, the initial fever pitch of the Spring-Heeled Jack panic inevitably subsided. The intense, almost nightly terror that had gripped London in 1838 gave way to a more sporadic and geographically diffuse pattern of sightings. Yet, Jack, or the idea of him, refused to vanish completely. He became a phantom woven into the fabric of Victorian Britain, a chilling whisper that could still, on occasion, manifest with startling clarity.

While many later reports were undoubtedly hoaxes, copycat pranks, or misidentifications amplified by the enduring legend, some incidents stood out, bearing the unsettling hallmarks of the original terror. One of the most compelling of these later accounts occurred far from the smog-choked streets of London, in the disciplined environment of Aldershot Barracks in 1877.

A sentry, on lonely night duty, reported a truly bizarre encounter. A strange figure, described as tall and clad in a glistening, tight-fitting suit, suddenly appeared before him, having apparently scaled a high wall with impossible ease. The figure, with eyes that shone red in the darkness, approached the sentry, who, despite his training, felt a primal fear grip him. When challenged, the entity did not speak but instead emitted a series of strange, guttural clicks. Then, it slapped the soldier's face several times – not with a human hand, the sentry insisted, but with something cold, hard, and claw-like. Before the stunned soldier could fully react or raise a more substantial alarm, the figure performed one of Spring-Heeled Jack's signature feats: it leaped, clearing an astonishing height and distance, vanishing back into the night as if it were no more substantial than smoke.

The Aldershot incident, reported by a soldier in a military setting, lent a renewed, albeit temporary, credibility to the idea that something genuinely inexplicable was still at large. Other scattered reports continued to surface throughout the mid to late 19th century – a shadowy figure leaping over rooftops in one town, a terrifying entity with glowing eyes frightening travellers on a lonely country road in another. Each instance would briefly reignite the old fears, the old questions.

However, the character of the sightings began to change. Spring-Heeled Jack was becoming less of an immediate, physical threat and more of a spectral bogeyman. The details grew less consistent, more folkloric. He was sometimes described as having horns and a tail, fully embracing the demonic aspect. His motives, always obscure, became even more nebulous. Was he a prankster? A demon? A visitor from some other realm? Or simply the product of collective anxiety given form?

The very name "Spring-Heeled Jack" became a convenient label for any unexplained nocturnal disturbance or peculiar assault. If a figure leaped an unusually high fence, if someone was frightened by a shadowy form in the dark, the cry of "Spring-Heeled Jack!" would invariably arise, often more out of ingrained habit than genuine belief in the original entity. He was transitioning from news to legend, his sharp, terrifying edges softened by time and retelling, yet his core mystery remained potent.

The gas lamps burned brighter, casting fewer deep shadows. Police forces became more organized, their methods more scientific. The world was, ostensibly, becoming a more rational, explainable place. Yet, the idea of Spring-Heeled Jack lingered, a testament to the unknown that lurked just beyond the encroaching light of modernity. He was the creature of the old, dark places, the embodiment of anxieties that reason could not entirely dispel. His active reign of terror might have been fading, his footsteps growing fainter in the annals of crime, but his leap into the darker corners of folklore was proving to be his most enduring feat of all. The man, or monster, was receding, but the chilling story, whispered from one generation to the next, was just beginning to solidify its hold.

As the 19th century yielded to the 20th, the tangible presence of Spring-Heeled Jack, if indeed it had ever been truly tangible, had all but evaporated. Yet, like an afterimage burned onto the retina, his legend persisted, flickering at the edges of public consciousness. There were still sporadic reports, though these became increasingly rare and often more easily dismissed. One of the last notable clusters of such "sightings" occurred in Liverpool in 1904, where a figure was seen leaping between rooftops, causing a brief local panic that echoed the great London scares of nearly seventy years prior. But these were faint echoes, ripples from a stone dropped long ago into a dark pond.

The mystery of Spring-Heeled Jack's true identity was never solved. No deathbed confession, no discovered costume or contraption, ever shed definitive light on the enigma. Was he the Marquess of Waterford, as many suspected, employing his wealth and derring-do for a series of outrageously cruel pranks? The timeline fits, to a degree, but some of the reported abilities stretch even the most generous interpretation of human capability. Was he a succession of copycats, each inspired by the terrifying original? Or was there something genuinely inexplicable, something that defied rational categorization, bounding through the gaslit nights of Victorian Britain? The questions hang in the air, unanswered, adding to the legend's enduring power.

What is undeniable is the profound impact Spring-Heeled Jack had on popular culture. He became a star of the penny dreadfuls, those cheap, sensationalist pamphlets devoured by a public hungry for thrills. On makeshift stages in dimly lit halls, melodramas depicted his terrifying exploits, often embellishing them with even more lurid details. He was cast as a villain, sometimes a tragic anti-hero, his distinctive silhouette – often imagined with bat-like wings or demonic horns in these later interpretations – becoming an instantly recognizable icon of Victorian dread. He burrowed deep into the British psyche, a uniquely unsettling bogeyman whose terror felt disturbingly real because, for a time, it was real to so many.

The tales of Spring-Heeled Jack serve as a potent reminder of a time when the urban landscape, even in the heart of a burgeoning empire, could still feel like a wilderness, a place where unknown entities might lurk just beyond the reach of the flickering gaslight. He represents the fear of the dark, the terror of the unknown attacker, the unsettling possibility that the familiar world can, in an instant, be rent by the inexplicable. His leaps defied not just gravity, but also easy explanation, lodging him firmly in that shadowy realm between hysteria and historical event.

To this day, the name Spring-Heeled Jack evokes a peculiar shiver. He is more than just a historical curiosity or a footnote in the annals of crime. He is an archetype, a manifestation of urban fear that adapted and evolved with the times but never entirely disappeared. The specifics of his appearance, the nature of his abilities, may blur and shift with each retelling, but the core image remains: a dark figure, capable of impossible feats, appearing from nowhere, spreading terror, and vanishing as if he were a figment of the collective nightmare.

Could such a figure exist? Could one man, or a series of men, truly perpetrate such acts and elude capture for so long? Or did the anxieties of a rapidly changing society coalesce into this singular, terrifying form? Perhaps the truth, like Jack himself, remains forever just out of reach, leaping across the rooftops of our imagination, a chilling enigma veiled in the enduring London fog. His story is a testament to the power of legend, a dark jewel in the crown of British folklore, ensuring that Spring-Heeled Jack, the terror of Victorian nights, will continue to leap through the shadows of our darkest tales for generations to come.

Cultural Insights

The tale of Spring-Heeled Jack is more than just a collection of bizarre assault reports from 19th-century Britain; it is a fascinating cultural artifact, a mirror reflecting the anxieties, social structures, and burgeoning media landscape of its time. To truly understand Jack's enduring grip on the popular imagination, we must delve into the fertile ground from which such a uniquely unsettling figure could spring.

The London of the 1830s, where Jack first made his terrifying debut, was a city undergoing immense transformation. The Industrial Revolution was reshaping not just the economy but the very fabric of society. Populations swelled as people flocked from the countryside seeking work, leading to overcrowded, often squalid living conditions in sprawling new suburbs. This rapid urbanization created a sense of anonymity previously unknown. Amongst the teeming, unfamiliar masses, who could truly know their neighbour? The new gas lighting, while celebrated as a marvel of progress, cast long, impenetrable shadows in the narrow alleyways and unlit courts, creating a stark chiaroscuro world where anything might lurk just beyond the pools of hesitant illumination. This was a city of stark contrasts – of visible progress and hidden squalor, of scientific advancement and lingering superstition – an environment ripe for the birth of a new kind of monster, one uniquely suited to the urban labyrinth.

Social anxieties were rife. Crime was a constant fear, particularly for women navigating the city alone. The stark class divisions of Victorian society also played a significant role. The theory that Spring-Heeled Jack was a "nobleman out on a cruel wager" – specifically targeting working-class women – resonated deeply. It tapped into existing resentments and suspicions about a decadent aristocracy perceived by some as being above the law, capable of indulging their whims at the expense of the vulnerable. Jack, in this light, became a symbol of aristocratic malice, a "wicked squire" archetype transplanted into the urban jungle.

The rise of the popular press was instrumental in Spring-

Heeled Jack's notoriety. Newspapers like The Times and later, the penny dreadfuls, seized upon the sensational aspects of the attacks. Detailed, often embellished, accounts of his glowing eyes, fiery breath, and incredible leaps fanned the flames of public fear and fascination. This was one of the first instances of a media-driven moral panic, where the reporting of events arguably amplified the phenomenon itself, possibly inspiring copycats or encouraging misinterpretation of ordinary events through the lens of the Jack hysteria. The very act of naming him "Spring-Heeled Jack" gave the disparate fears a concrete, easily transmissible identity.

Folklore traditions undoubtedly contributed to the public's interpretation of Jack. His demonic attributes – the fiery breath, glowing eyes, and sometimes (in later accounts) horns and a tail – aligned with long-standing images of devils and mischievous, malevolent spirits. His incredible agility echoed tales of nimble tricksters or supernatural beings capable of defying human limitations. He became a "folk devil," a personification of societal anxieties, much like older bogeymen who served to warn against straying from the path or venturing into dangerous places after dark.

The psychological impact of Jack's reported abilities cannot be overstated. In an age that increasingly prided itself on reason and scientific understanding, his seemingly supernatural feats – particularly the prodigious leaps and the reported ability to spit blue flames – were profoundly unsettling. These acts defied easy explanation, pushing the boundaries of perceived reality. This very inexplicability was key to his terror and his longevity as a legend. Had he simply been a masked ruffian, he might have been caught or faded into the annals of common crime. But the uncanny nature of his reported actions elevated him, suggesting something beyond the merely human.

Even the technology of the era, or rather anxieties and fascinations surrounding it, may have played a part. Some theories suggested Jack used hidden springs in his boots or some sort of bellows mechanism for his flames. This reflects a society grappling with new inventions and the sometimes-unsettling potential of mechanical contrivances. The idea that human ingenuity could be twisted to such terrifying ends was, in itself, a modern fear.

Spring-Heeled Jack's legacy is significant. He is often cited as a precursor to pulp heroes and villains, an early example of a costumed figure with extraordinary abilities operating outside the law. His influence can be seen in the DNA of characters who leap across rooftops, whether for good or ill. More broadly, he cemented a particular type of urban legend: the elusive, terror-inducing figure who haunts cityscapes, embodying the hidden dangers and anxieties of modern life.

The enduring question, of course, is who or what Spring-Heeled Jack truly was. The lack of a definitive answer is perhaps the most crucial element of his lasting power. Was he one individual, a series of pranksters, a manifestation of mass hysteria, or something else entirely? Each theory has its proponents and its holes. This ambiguity allows each generation to reinterpret Jack, to project onto him their own contemporary fears.

Ultimately, Spring-Heeled Jack remains a potent symbol. He is a chilling reminder that even in our most civilized spaces, the inexplicable can erupt, that fear can spread like wildfire, and that some mysteries may never be solved, destined to leap forever through the shadowy alleyways of our collective imagination. His story is not just about what happened, but about what could happen, tapping into that primal unease that lurks just beneath the surface of our ordered world.

The Beast of Bodmin Moor

B odmin Moor. The very name conjures images of a vast, untamed expanse in the heart of Cornwall, a landscape of stark beauty and brooding desolation. Granite tors, ancient and weather-beaten, thrust upwards like the exposed bones of the land, their silhouettes stark against often-leaden skies. Heather and gorse cling to the thin soil, painting the moor in hues of purple and gold, but also concealing treacherous bogs and forgotten mine workings. It is a place steeped in history, littered with prehistoric stone circles, quoits, and hut circles – remnants of peoples who lived and died here millennia ago, their stories absorbed into the very peat and granite. This is a land that feels ancient, a place where the veil between worlds can seem thin, where the wind carries whispers of things unseen.

For generations, the moor has been the domain of hardy

sheep and ponies, of farmers who carved a living from its challenging terrain. And for just as long, there have been stories. Not always of a great cat, not at first. But there were always tales of the moor's mysteries – of strange lights, of unexplained disappearances, of the feeling of being watched when supposedly alone amongst the silent tors. It was a landscape that invited such speculation, that seemed to hold its secrets close.

Then, slowly, almost imperceptibly at first, a new kind of whisper began to circulate. Throughout the mid to late 20th century, sporadic reports surfaced. A motorist driving a lonely road at dusk would catch a fleeting glimpse of something large and dark slinking through the bracken. A farmer might find a sheep inexplicably savaged, the kill too clean for a fox, too powerful for a domestic dog. These were isolated incidents, often dismissed as misidentification – a large feral dog, a deer seen in poor light, perhaps even the product of an overactive imagination fueled by the moor's inherent eeriness. There was no pattern, no cohesive narrative, just scattered anecdotes that would flare up briefly in local pubs or village shops before fading back into the background hum of rural life.

By the early 1980s, however, these whispers started to gain a little more substance, a little more frequency. The anecdotal evidence began to mount. More farmers reported unusual livestock kills. The wounds were often deep, suggestive of a powerful predator with formidable claws and teeth. Sometimes, carcasses were found partially eaten, dragged considerable distances, or even, unsettlingly, cached as if the killer intended to return. These weren't the messy, opportunistic kills of smaller predators; these spoke of something larger, something more methodical.

Eyewitness accounts, though still infrequent and often fleeting, started to paint a more consistent, if deeply unsettling, picture. People spoke of seeing a large, cat-like creature, bigger than any known native British wild animal, save perhaps for the Scottish Wildcat, and this was something else entirely. Descriptions varied slightly, as eyewitness accounts often do under stress and in poor visibility, but common themes emerged: a creature the size of a large dog, perhaps a Labrador or an Alsatian, but with distinctly feline characteristics – a long, sinuous body, a sleek, dark coat (often black or very dark brown), a lengthy, curling tail, and an unnervingly silent, predatory grace. Some mentioned luminous eyes caught in headlights, a chilling green or yellow glow that seemed to hang in the darkness for a moment before vanishing.

These were not yet the banner headlines they would become, but a low thrum of unease was building within the scattered communities that bordered and dotted the moor. The old tales of the moor's strangeness were being augmented by something new, something that felt more tangible, more threatening. The land itself, with its vast, uninhabited stretches and dense cover, offered a perfect refuge for such an elusive creature. If something truly wild and out of place had been released, or had found its way onto Bodmin Moor, it could thrive there, unseen for the most part, its presence only betrayed by the occasional chilling glimpse or the grim discovery of a freshly slain ewe. The moor was keeping its secrets, but the whispers were growing louder, hinting at a formidable, unknown predator stalking its ancient, granite heart.

As the 1980s gave way to the 1990s, the low thrum of unease surrounding Bodmin Moor began to escalate into a palpable wave of fear and frustration. What had once been sporadic whispers and isolated incidents intensified, transforming into a consistent pattern of unsettling sightings and, more alarmingly, devastating livestock losses. The term "Beast of Bodmin Moor" started to appear with increasing regularity in local newspapers and on regional news broadcasts, no longer a mere curiosity but a recognized and deeply worrying phenomenon.

The eyewitness accounts grew in number and clarity. Farmers, walkers, and motorists – ordinary people going about their daily lives – reported encounters that left them shaken and profoundly disturbed. The descriptions solidified: a large, powerful cat, consistently reported as being between three and five feet in length, with a long, thick tail. Its coat was almost always described as black or exceptionally dark brown, sleek and glossy, like that of a panther. Its movements were cited as undeniably feline – fluid, silent, and imbued with a predatory grace that sent shivers down the spines of those who observed it, even from a distance. Some spoke of its powerful musculature, visible even beneath its dark fur; others recalled the unnerving intensity of its gaze when its eyes, often described as yellowish-green, were caught in torchlight or headlamps.

These weren't fleeting glimpses of something ambiguous in the twilight anymore. People reported seeing the creature for extended periods, sometimes observing it stalking prey, other times finding themselves unexpectedly face-to-face with it on a lonely moorland track. The sheer consistency of these independent reports, coming from credible individuals across different parts of the moor and its surrounding areas, made it increasingly difficult to dismiss the phenomenon as mere misidentification or hysteria.

But it was the livestock kills that truly brought the crisis to a head. The attacks became more frequent, more brutal. Farmers would discover sheep, lambs, and sometimes even calves, slain in a manner that defied easy explanation. The kills were often clean, with deep puncture wounds to the neck or throat, indicative of a predator that knew precisely how to dispatch its prey. Carcasses were frequently found disemboweled with an almost surgical precision, organs selectively consumed. Sometimes, only the head and skin would remain. The sheer force suggested by the injuries, the way animals were sometimes dragged significant distances, pointed to something far more powerful than a fox or a feral dog.

The economic impact on the local farming community was significant. Each lost animal was a blow to their livelihood. But beyond the financial cost, there was a growing sense of siege, of helplessness. These were people who understood the land, who knew its natural inhabitants, and this was something alien, something outside their experience. The psychological toll was immense. Farmers spoke of sleepless nights, of the dread of what they might find in their fields at dawn. Children were warned to be wary, and a shadow of fear fell over communities that had long felt a sense of security in their rural isolation. The moor, once a familiar, if sometimes harsh, neighbour, now felt like a place that harbored a hidden, malevolent secret.

Local newspapers were filled with accounts. One farmer near St Austell reported losing over twenty lambs in a single season, each one bearing the hallmarks of the mystery predator. Another, closer to Bodmin itself, described finding a ewe with its throat ripped out, its body strangely untouched otherwise, as if killed for sport or by a creature interrupted. The sheer scale of the problem began to attract national media attention, and the Beast of Bodmin Moor became a household name across Britain. Scepticism remained in some quarters, particularly from afar, but for those living in the shadow of the moor, the threat was all too real. The shadows of Bodmin held a genuine terror, and the slaughter in the fields was undeniable proof that something wild, powerful, and utterly out of place was stalking the ancient Cornish landscape. The calls for official investigation and action grew from a concerned murmur to an insistent roar.

The escalating fear and the mounting toll of livestock losses could not be ignored indefinitely. By the mid-1990s, the clamour from farmers, concerned residents, and even some local politicians for an official inquiry into the Beast of Bodmin Moor reached a crescendo. The government, under pressure to address what was becoming a significant rural issue and a media sensation, finally tasked the Ministry of Agriculture, Fisheries and Food (MAFF) with conducting a formal investigation. The findings, released in 1995, were awaited with bated breath by many.

The MAFF investigation was, by its nature, a methodical and scientific undertaking. Experts were dispatched to Bodmin Moor. They interviewed witnesses, examined livestock carcasses, took casts of alleged pugmarks, collected samples of droppings, and scrutinised the scant photographic and video material that had emerged. The aim was to determine, with as much certainty as possible, whether a "big cat" or an unidentified predator was indeed at large and responsible for the widespread claims.

The evidence, however, proved stubbornly elusive and frustratingly ambiguous. Pugmarks, while sometimes large and suggestive of a cat, were often found in conditions that made definitive identification difficult – rain-washed soil, soft peat, or partial prints. Some could be attributed to large dogs, others remained tantalizingly inconclusive. Droppings, or scats, when analysed, often revealed the remains of common prey like rabbits, but rarely offered irrefutable proof of a panther or puma. Hair samples were equally problematic, often turning out to be from known domestic or wild animals.

The photographic and video evidence that had surfaced was, for the most part, blurry, distant, or too fleeting to provide conclusive proof. A dark shape moving against a distant hillside, a pair of glowing eyes in the night – these images fueled speculation but fell short of the scientific rigour required for official confirmation. The very nature of Bodmin Moor, with its vast, difficult terrain and unpredictable weather, made systematic tracking or the clear capture of such an elusive creature an almost impossible task. The Beast, if it existed, seemed to possess an uncanny ability to avoid definitive detection.

Then came a moment that briefly seemed to promise a breakthrough. In December 1995, shortly after the official MAFF report was published, a young boy discovered a large, leopard-like skull near the River Fowey on the edges of Bodmin Moor. The skull was undeniably feline and appeared to belong to a juvenile leopard. For a moment, it seemed like tangible proof. The media seized upon the discovery: "Beast of Bodmin Skull Found!" screamed the headlines. Could this be it? The physical remnant of the elusive creature, or perhaps one of its offspring?

The excitement, however, was short-lived. Closer examination by experts at the Natural History Museum in London revealed a less sensational truth. The skull was indeed that of a young male leopard, but it showed clear signs of having been imported as part of a leopard-skin rug. There were cut marks on the back, and it had been stored in conditions inconsistent with having lain exposed on the moor for any significant length of time. It was, most likely, a hoax or a discarded item with no direct connection to the alleged living Beast.

The official MAFF report itself concluded that there was "no verifiable evidence" of exotic felines at large on Bodmin Moor and that severe weather conditions and attacks by native predators or dogs were likely responsible for most livestock losses. While acknowledging the sincerity of many eyewitnesses, the report suggested that "the occurrence of a 'mystery cat' has been comprehensively exaggerated."

This conclusion was met with a mixed reaction. For sceptics, it confirmed their belief that the Beast was a product of misidentification and rural myth-making. For many locals, particularly the farmers who had suffered losses and the individuals who had witnessed the creature firsthand, the official findings felt like a dismissal of their experiences. They knew what they had seen, and the neat, bureaucratic explanations did little to dispel their conviction that something very real, and very dangerous, still roamed the moor. The hunt for evidence had, in many ways, deepened the mystery rather than solving it, drawing a line between official pronouncements and deeply entrenched local belief. The moor, it seemed, was not yet ready to give up its secrets.

The official MAFF report of 1995, with its assertion of "no verifiable evidence," might have been expected to lay the legend of the Beast of Bodmin Moor to rest. For a time, perhaps it did dampen the wider national fervor. The media spotlight, always hungry for novelty, began to drift towards other curiosities. Yet, on Bodmin Moor itself, and in the surrounding towns and villages of Cornwall, the story was far from over. The Beast, it seemed, was not so easily banished by bureaucratic ink.

Sightings, though perhaps less intensely publicized, continued. Individuals – locals and visitors alike – still reported fleeting glimpses of a large, dark, cat-like creature moving with silent grace across the desolate landscape or darting across a remote road in the dead of night. Livestock kills, while sometimes attributed to more conventional causes, occasionally bore those unsettling hallmarks that reignited old fears and suspicions. The Beast had, in a sense, gone deeper underground, becoming a more elusive, almost spectral presence, but one that resolutely refused to disappear from the local consciousness.

Over the years, the Beast of Bodmin Moor has become inextricably woven into the tapestry of modern Cornish folklore. It has evolved from a headline-grabbing menace into an enigmatic icon, a symbol of the wild, untamed spirit of Cornwall's ancient heartland. The creature now features in local art, literature, and even has a somewhat tongue-in-cheek presence in the tourist trade, with "Beast" memorabilia and themed attractions appearing. This cultural assimilation, however, does not necessarily negate the genuine belief held by many that something real underpins the legend. For some, it's a way of processing and living alongside an unsettling possibility.

The theories about its origin continue to circulate, each offering a potential explanation for the persistent sightings. The most widely accepted, and perhaps most plausible, is that the Beast, or beasts, are descendants of exotic big cats – pumas, panthers, or leopards – that were released or escaped from private collections, particularly around the time the Dangerous Wild Animals Act of 1976 came into force, making it more difficult and expensive to keep such animals. The argument goes that the remote and rugged terrain of Bodmin Moor provided a suitable, isolated habitat where such creatures could survive and even breed, largely undetected.

Other theories suggest misidentification of exceptionally large domestic cats gone feral, or even of native species like the Scottish Wildcat, though the latter is not officially recognized as having a presence so far south. More esoteric explanations, though less common, sometimes surface, hinting at something beyond the purely zoological – a guardian spirit of the moor, or a creature of even more mysterious provenance, echoing the land's ancient, pre-Christian past.

What remains undeniable is the power of the unknown. Bodmin Moor, with its vast, often-shrouded expanses and its deep sense of history, is a landscape perfectly suited to harboring secrets. The lack of definitive proof, rather than killing the legend, seems to nourish it. It allows the Beast to exist in that liminal space between fact and folklore, a creature of both the physical world and the collective imagination.

Perhaps the truth is complex. Maybe there were, at one point, one or more escaped exotic cats. Perhaps some sightings are indeed misidentifications. And perhaps, too, the power of suggestion and the deep-seated human fascination with the idea of a hidden predator in our midst play their part. The Beast of Bodmin Moor serves as a potent reminder that even in our modern, technologically advanced world, there are still wild places, and within them, mysteries that resist easy explanation.

The moor continues to keep its counsel. The wind still sighs across the granite tors, carrying whispers that may, or may not, be of a sleek, dark form moving silently through the heather. And so, the Beast endures – a shadow on the periphery, a question mark in the wild heart of Cornwall, a testament to the enduring allure of the unexplained and the wildness that can linger just beyond the edges of our understanding.

Cultural Insights

The legend of the Beast of Bodmin Moor is far more than a simple tale of an out-of-place predator; it is a rich narrative woven from the threads of a unique landscape, deep-seated human anxieties, the dynamics of modern media, and the resilient power of local belief in the face of official skepticism. To truly appreciate its resonance, one must look beyond the disputed pugmarks and blurry photographs and explore the cultural ecosystem in which this enigmatic creature found its footing.

At the heart of the legend lies Bodmin Moor itself. This expanse of granite upland is not merely a backdrop but an active participant in the story. Its ancient, often desolate beauty, its history stretching back to pre-Roman times, and its frequently-shrouded, isolated character create an atmosphere ripe for secrets and speculation. The moor is a palimpsest of human endeavour and natural wildness, littered with Neolithic stone circles, Bronze Age hut remnants, and the stark ruins of a more recent mining industry. It's a place where the past feels tangibly present, and the vast, often featureless tracts can easily play tricks on the eye and mind. Such landscapes have always been fertile ground for folklore, for tales of mysterious denizens and unexplained occurrences. The moor provides not just a plausible habitat for an elusive creature, but also a psychological space where the extraordinary can seem possible.

The Beast of Bodmin Moor is arguably the most famous manifestation of a wider phenomenon in Britain: "Alien Big Cat" (ABC) sightings. Reports of large, non-native felines roaming the countryside have surfaced from Kent to Scotland, with "phantom panthers," "putative pumas," and "lurking leopards" becoming recurring motifs in local news and folklore across the nation. A common thread in many ABC theories is the Dangerous Wild Animals Act of 1976. This legislation imposed stricter regulations and licensing requirements for keeping exotic animals. It is widely speculated that some owners, unwilling or unable to comply with the new laws, may have illicitly released their creatures into the wild. The remote and rugged parts of Britain, like Bodmin Moor, would have seemed ideal, if irresponsible, locations for such releases.

The media played an undeniable role in shaping the Beast of Bodmin Moor narrative. Local newspapers initially, and later national outlets, amplified the accounts of sightings and livestock kills. While this brought much-needed attention to the plight of farmers, it also, at times, veered into sensationalism. The "Beast" became a compelling story, a modern mystery unfolding in real-time. This intense media scrutiny helped cement the legend in the public consciousness, but it also created a feedback loop where any unusual event on or near the moor could be readily attributed to the Beast, sometimes with little concrete evidence. This is a classic element in the formation of modern myths – the interplay between genuine experiences, media portrayal, and public perception.

For the farming communities around Bodmin Moor, the Beast was no abstract cryptid; it was a tangible threat with severe economic and psychological repercussions. The loss of livestock, often in brutal and inexplicable ways, caused genuine hardship and distress. The feeling of helplessness in the face of an unseen, powerful predator, and the initial struggle to have these concerns taken seriously by authorities, fostered a strong sense of local solidarity and a conviction rooted in firsthand experience. This grassroots belief, born of tangible loss and unsettling encounters, has always been a powerful counterweight to official skepticism.

The 1995 MAFF investigation and its conclusion of "no verifiable evidence" highlighted this tension. While the scientific approach sought definitive proof, which remained elusive, it often felt dismissive to those who believed they had seen the creature or its handiwork. The infamous "Beast of Bodmin skull," initially hailed as potential proof only to be debunked as an imported leopard-skin rug component, became a focal point of this dynamic – a symbol of the frustrating search for truth and the ease with which hopes could be raised and dashed. It underscored the difficulty of applying purely scientific methods to a phenomenon that also encompassed elements of eyewitness testimony, local knowledge, and deeply ingrained belief.

In the years since the peak hysteria, the Beast of Bodmin Moor has become deeply embedded in Cornish cultural identity. It has transcended its status as a mere news story to become a piece of contemporary folklore, a local legend that contributes to the region's unique mystique. Tourist shops sell Beast-themed memorabilia, and the legend often features in local storytelling and art. This cultural assimilation demonstrates the power of such stories to capture the imagination and become part of a place's narrative, even if their factual basis remains contested.

At its core, the Beast of Bodmin Moor taps into primal human fears and fascinations. The idea of a large, unseen predator lurking just beyond the fringes of our settled world speaks to an ancient anxiety. In an increasingly tamed and understood landscape, the thought that something wild and inexplicable might still roam free is both unsettling and strangely alluring. The Beast represents a pocket of irreducible wildness, a question mark against the backdrop of our ordered lives.

The enduring nature of the legend is, in many ways, fueled by the lack of definitive resolution. If the Beast were definitively proven to exist, or conclusively proven not to, the story would lose much of its power. It is the ambiguity, the "what if?", that keeps it alive. The Beast of Bodmin Moor thus remains a compelling example of a living legend, reflecting our complex relationship with the natural world, the mysteries it holds, and the enduring human need to tell stories that explore the shadowy borderlands between the known and the unknown.

The Highgate Vampire

Highgate Cemetery, sprawling across a leafy hillside in North London, is more than just a burial ground; it is a city of the dead, a breathtaking testament to Victorian England's elaborate mourning customs and its fascination with the gothic. Consecrated in 1839, its older Western side, in particular, became a labyrinth of ivy-strangled angels, crumbling mausoleums, and shadowed catacombs, their grandeur slowly succumbing to decades of neglect by the late 1960s. Ornate tombs, once proud monuments to wealthy merchants and esteemed artists, now sagged under the weight of time and encroaching nature, their stone surfaces stained dark by London's damp air. It was a place of profound, melancholic beauty, a silent, slumbering metropolis of the departed that seemed to exist outside the thrum of the modern city that surrounded it.

But within these decaying splendours, a new kind of disquiet began to stir. By the latter half of the 1960s, tales started to circulate amongst those who lived near the cemetery or dared to wander its overgrown paths. Visitors spoke of sudden, inexplicable drops in temperature, of feeling an unseen presence watching them from the deeper shadows, of an overwhelming sense of dread that would descend without warning. Some claimed to hear faint whispers or rustling sounds emanating from within sealed tombs. More disturbingly, a few reported fleeting glimpses of a tall, dark figure, often described as having a spectral, almost unnaturally greyish pallor, that would vanish silently amongst the gravestones if approached.

These were, initially, the kind of stories that often attach themselves to old cemeteries – attributed to overactive imaginations, the play of light and shadow, or the natural eeriness of such a place. The cemetery, largely unkempt and poorly secured, had also become a haunt for vandals and those drawn to its romantic desolation for less than reverent purposes.

However, in late 1969, these vague anxieties began to coalesce around a more focused narrative, largely thanks to the efforts of one young man: David Farrant. Farrant, president of the fledgling British Psychic and Occult Society, had developed a keen interest in the strange reports emanating from Highgate. He began conducting his own nocturnal investigations within the cemetery's Western side, often accompanied by a female companion. In December 1969, he wrote a letter to the Hampstead & Highgate Express, a local newspaper, detailing his experiences. He described encountering what he termed a "grey figure," which he believed to be some form of supernatural entity, possibly a ghost or elemental, that seemed to drain psychic energy from its surroundings. He spoke of its appearance being "tall and dark," and of the tangible coldness that accompanied its manifestations. Farrant also mentioned that he and his companion had seen foxes dead in the cemetery with no visible injuries, only small marks on their throats.

Farrant's letter, and his subsequent interviews, struck a chord. Others came forward with their own unsettling tales. One young woman recounted being knocked to the ground by a dark shape with "burning eyes" as she walked past the cemetery gates late one night. Another witness described a figure that seemed to glide rather than walk, its face obscured by shadow, disappearing into the wall of a mausoleum. The stories, though varied in their specifics, shared a common thread of a tall, shadowy presence that exuded an aura of menace and unnatural cold.

The local press, sensing a good story, began to give these accounts increasing prominence. The "Highgate Ghost" or the "Highgate Horror" became a topic of local conversation. At this stage, the word "vampire" had not yet dominated the discourse, but the elements were there: a spectral entity, an atmosphere of dread, and unexplained animal deaths. The whispers from the tombs of Highgate were growing louder, setting the stage for a far more dramatic and sensational interpretation of the unfolding mystery. The cemetery, with its crumbling grandeur and aura of decay, was proving to be the perfect theatre for a modern gothic horror story to begin.

David Farrant's sober, if unsettling, accounts of a "grey figure" haunting Highgate Cemetery might have remained a local curiosity, a minor ghost story for the North London suburbs. However, the narrative took a sharp, theatrical turn with the arrival of another self-styled occult investigator: Seán Manchester. Manchester, a younger man who presented himself as a bishop in a little-known esoteric Christian church and the president of the British Occult Society (a distinct entity from Farrant's group), had also taken an interest in the Highgate phenomena. In February 1970, following Farrant's initial letters and media appearances, Manchester offered his own, far more sensational, interpretation to the Hampstead & Highgate Express.

Where Farrant had spoken cautiously of a spectral entity, Manchester declared with authority that Highgate Cemetery was haunted by nothing less than a "King Vampire of the Undead." He claimed this vampire was a nobleman, a practitioner of black magic from Wallachia, Romania, who had been transported to England in his coffin in the 18th century and interred on the site where Highgate Cemetery was later built. This vampire, Manchester asserted, had been roused from its slumber by modern Satanists performing rituals within the cemetery grounds. He painted a vivid picture of a creature of immense evil, possessing supernatural strength and a thirst for blood, responsible not only for the unsettling atmosphere but also for the drained animal carcasses – foxes and domestic pets – that were reportedly being found in and around the cemetery, their throats bearing tell-tale puncture marks.

Manchester's pronouncements, steeped in classic vampire lore and delivered with an air of confident expertise, were perfectly tailored for media consumption. The word "vampire," with its rich, dark connotations, immediately captured the public imagination in a way Farrant's "grey figure" had not. Newspapers, particularly the more sensationalist tabloids, seized upon the story with relish. Headlines screamed of the

"Highgate Vampire," and the narrative rapidly escalated from a local ghost story to a full-blown vampire scare.

A public rivalry quickly developed between Farrant and Manchester. Farrant, while acknowledging the sinister nature of the entity, maintained his belief that it was a more elemental or ghostly presence, not necessarily a blood-sucking vampire in the traditional sense. He accused Manchester of sensationalizing the situation and potentially endangering the public with his dramatic claims. Manchester, in turn, dismissed Farrant as an amateur, lacking the true esoteric knowledge required to understand or combat such a powerful undead entity. Their conflicting views and mutual criticisms were eagerly reported by the press, adding another layer of drama to the unfolding saga. Each man seemed to court media attention, granting interviews and posing for photographs in the atmospheric surroundings of Highgate Cemetery, often with crucifixes or other occult paraphernalia.

The public fear, fanned by the escalating media reports and the pronouncements of the rival occultists, grew tangible. Residents near the cemetery reported disturbed sleep, nightmares, and an increasing sense of unease. The tales of drained animals, whether entirely accurate or amplified by panic, lent a horrifying credence to the vampire theory. People spoke of seeing the tall, dark figure with greater frequency, its eyes now often described as "hypnotic" or "blazing red." The cemetery, once a place of melancholic beauty, was fast becoming, in the public mind, a lairs of unspeakable evil. The stage was being set for a confrontation, a desperate attempt by ordinary people and self-proclaimed experts alike to confront the darkness that seemed to have taken root amongst the ancient tombs of Highgate. The whispers had become a roar, and the city was holding its breath.

The escalating media frenzy and the increasingly dire warnings from Seán Manchester, who claimed the Highgate Vampire was gaining power and that official inaction was perilous, created an atmosphere of intense anticipation and barely suppressed panic. Manchester, in television interviews broadcast in early March 1970, spoke of the necessity of locating and destroying the vampire by traditional means: staking it through the heart, beheading it, and burning its remains. He hinted that he knew the location of the vampire's tomb and planned to conduct an exorcism. While he urged the public not to interfere, his pronouncements, coupled with the sensationalist press coverage, inadvertently set the stage for an extraordinary and chaotic event.

The chosen date for Manchester's proposed exorcism, whether explicitly stated by him or simply inferred by an agitated public, became fixed in many minds: Friday, March 13th, 1970. The confluence of a traditionally unlucky day with the promise of a climactic confrontation with a supposed creature of darkness proved an irresistible lure for a public primed by weeks of vampire hysteria.

As dusk began to settle over London on that infamous Friday, an unprecedented scene began to unfold around the perimeter of Highgate Cemetery. What started as a trickle of curious onlookers soon swelled into a crowd, then a mob. Hundreds of people – teenagers, thrill-seekers, concerned locals, amateur occultists, and those simply swept up in the moment – converged on Swain's Lane, the main thoroughfare bordering the cemetery. They came armed not just with morbid curiosity, but with makeshift weapons: wooden stakes hastily fashioned from broken fences or chair legs, crucifixes clutched in nervous hands, garlic, and even knives. It was a scene that seemed ripped from the pages of a Victorian penny dreadful, a medieval witch-hunt transplanted into the heart of 20th-century London.

Ignoring the cemetery's locked gates and high walls, and fueled by a potent cocktail of fear, excitement, and mob mentality, the crowd surged forward. They clambered over the iron railings, scaled the lichen-covered brickwork, and poured into the labyrinthine Western Cemetery. The air was thick with shouts, nervous laughter, and the sound of running feet. Torches and flashlights cut erratic beams through the darkness, casting grotesque, dancing shadows upon the ancient tombs and weather-beaten angels.

The scene inside the cemetery descended into chaos. Groups of self-styled vampire hunters, many with no clear idea of what they were looking for or what they would do if they found it, fanned out through the overgrown pathways. They peered into shadowed mausoleums, tugged at the doors of ancient vaults, and shouted challenges to the unseen entity. The atmosphere was a bizarre mixture of carnival and crusade, a mass trespass fueled by superstition and media hype. The delicate, decaying beauty of Highgate was trampled underfoot as the mob, emboldened by numbers, sought their quarry.

The police, initially caught off guard by the scale of the invasion, struggled to restore order. Officers found themselves confronted by a horde of excited, often irrational, individuals convinced they were participating in a righteous, if terrifying, quest. It took hours to clear the cemetery, to coax and cajole the would-be hunters back over the walls and out into the streets. Miraculously, amidst the pandemonium, no serious injuries were reported, though the cemetery itself bore the scars of the night's intrusion.

The great Highgate Vampire hunt of March 13th, 1970, found no vampire. No "King of the Undead" was dragged from his lair to face the stakes and torches of the London mob. But the event itself became legendary. It was a stark, almost unbelievable demonstration of how ancient fears, amplified by modern media and championed by charismatic personalities, could overwhelm reason and lead to mass public hysteria. The night cemented the Highgate Vampire in the annals of urban legend, transforming it from a local spook story into an international sensation, a cautionary tale of how easily the veneer of modern rationality can be stripped away to reveal the primal fears that lurk beneath.

The chaotic spectacle of the March 13th vampire hunt did not, as one might expect, put an end to the Highgate saga. Instead, it seemed to entrench the key players in their positions and usher in a new, stranger phase of the legend, one marked by increasingly bizarre claims, occult rivalries, and a disturbing pattern of desecration within Highgate Cemetery itself.

In the immediate aftermath of the hunt, both David Farrant and Seán Manchester claimed that the vampire had not been found or destroyed by the mob. Each asserted that they alone possessed the knowledge and ability to deal with the entity. Manchester, in particular, maintained that he had entered the cemetery on various occasions, located the vampire's tomb (the precise location of which he kept a closely guarded secret), and performed rites of exorcism, including driving a stake through what he claimed was the vampire's corpse. He would later publish photographs purporting to show these activities, though their authenticity was, like much in this case, hotly debated.

Farrant, meanwhile, continued his own investigations, often

claiming to have encountered the "grey figure" or other malevolent presences. He reported being psychically attacked and experiencing poltergeist-like phenomena, which he attributed to the Highgate entity or perhaps to darker forces stirred up by the ongoing events. He was arrested multiple times within the cemetery, sometimes for vandalism or disturbing graves, charges he often attributed to his attempts to investigate or neutralize supernatural threats.

The cemetery, already suffering from neglect, became a focal point for more sinister activities. Reports of genuine occult rituals, vandalism, and even the desecration of tombs continued throughout the early 1970s. Coffins were broken open, bodies disturbed, and strange symbols sometimes found daubed on mausoleums. While it was difficult to ascertain direct links between these acts and the two main protagonists of the vampire affair, the atmosphere of supernatural dread and the public notoriety of the cemetery undoubtedly attracted individuals with morbid or destructive intent. The authorities struggled to secure the vast, labyrinthine grounds.

The rivalry between Farrant and Manchester intensified, descending into a bitter and highly public feud. They traded insults and accusations in the press and through their own publications. Each man positioned himself as the true expert, the genuine defender against the supernatural, while casting the other as a charlatan, a fraud, or even a dangerous dabbler in the dark arts.

This animosity culminated in one of the most peculiar episodes of the entire affair: an alleged "magickal duel" between the two men. In April 1973, Farrant claimed that Manchester had challenged him to a duel to the death on Parliament Hill, overlooking Highgate Cemetery. According to Farrant, he attended, but Manchester failed to appear. Manchester's version of events, naturally, differed. He later claimed to have confronted and bested Farrant on a different occasion, using psychic powers to protect himself from Farrant's supposed malevolent intentions. Regardless of the "truth" of these claims – which seemed to exist more in the realm of theatrical pronouncement than verifiable event – the story of the wizards' duel added another layer of bizarre melodrama to the legend.

The Highgate Vampire story, which had begun with whispered fears and a shadowy figure, had now become deeply entangled with the personalities and public personas of these two rival occultists. Their ongoing conflict, played out in newspaper columns and television interviews, often overshadowed the original mystery of what, if anything, truly haunted Highgate Cemetery. The vampire itself seemed almost secondary to the human drama, a drama that saw both men face legal troubles and public scrutiny for their activities and claims related to the cemetery and its alleged unholy resident. The shadow of the vampire had indeed grown long, casting a pall not just over Highgate's ancient tombs, but also over the lives and reputations of those who claimed to hunt it.

As the 1970s wore on, the intense, almost feverish public obsession with the Highgate Vampire gradually began to wane. The sensational headlines became less frequent, and the dramatic pronouncements of David Farrant and Seán Manchester, while still occasionally surfacing, no longer commanded the same widespread media attention. The immediate panic, the thrill of the hunt, and the bizarre theatre of occult rivalries started to fade into the background noise of a city preoccupied with more contemporary concerns.

Yet, the Highgate Vampire did not simply vanish. Its shadow, once cast so sharply by the glare of media frenzy, stretched long and deep, becoming permanently etched into the folklore of London and the annals of modern urban legends. The events of the early 1970s, particularly the infamous mass vampire hunt, had ensured its notoriety. Highgate Cemetery itself, its gothic beauty now tinged with a darker reputation, became inextricably linked with the tale. Efforts were made to improve security, to protect its fragile monuments from further vandalism, and to manage the influx of curiosity-seekers drawn by its macabre fame. The Friends of Highgate Cemetery, formed in 1975, took on the crucial role of preserving and protecting this historic site, gradually restoring its dignity while acknowledging its unique and sometimes unsettling past.

Looking back, the Highgate Vampire affair serves as a fascinating case study in how modern myths are made. It was a potent concoction: an atmospheric, neglected Victorian cemetery providing the perfect gothic stage; genuine, if initially vague, reports of unsettling experiences; the arrival of charismatic individuals offering dramatic, supernatural explanations; and a media landscape eager for sensational content. The rivalry between Farrant and Manchester, while often descending into acrimony and questionable claims, undeniably fueled the narrative, providing ongoing conflict and intrigue that the press readily exploited. The very human elements of belief, fear, personal ambition, and public suggestibility all played their parts.

The phenomenon can be seen as a classic moral panic, where societal anxieties – perhaps about changing social norms, the perceived rise of occultism, or simply a primal fear of the unknown – coalesced around a specific, identifiable threat. The vampire, an age-old symbol of predatory evil and forbidden desires, provided a powerful and readily understandable framework for these fears. The reported animal mutilations, whether directly linked or not, lent a visceral, gruesome edge to the story, making the threat seem horribly tangible.

The question of what, if anything, truly haunted Highgate Cemetery in the late 1960s remains open to speculation. Were the initial sightings of a "grey figure" genuine encounters with some unexplained phenomenon – a localised haunting, an elemental presence, or something else entirely – that was later hijacked and reinterpreted through the lens of vampire mythology? Or was the entire affair a product of misidentification, delusion, and media hype from the outset? The truth likely lies somewhere in the complex interplay of these factors. The power of suggestion, especially when amplified by authoritative-sounding pronouncements and widespread media coverage, can be immense.

Today, the Highgate Vampire is more a piece of dark heritage than an active source of panic. It's a story told on ghost tours, debated in online forums, and dissected in books on folklore and the paranormal. It stands as a testament to the enduring allure of vampire mythology, even in a supposedly rational, secular age. It reminds us that beneath the surface of modern urban life, ancient fears and archetypes can still exert a powerful hold, particularly when nurtured by the right combination of place, personality, and publicity.

The tombs of Highgate now rest in greater peace, watched over and cared for. Yet, the legend lingers, a whisper amongst the ivy and the angels. The Highgate Vampire may never have been caught, staked, or definitively proven, but it has achieved a different kind of immortality – that of a truly unforgettable urban legend, a chilling reminder of a time when North London believed itself to be under siege from the undead.

Cultural Insights

The Highgate Vampire affair of the late 1960s and early 1970s stands as a remarkable case study in the birth and evolution of a modern urban legend. Unlike ancient folktales whispered across generations, this terror unfolded under the bright lights of television cameras and the bold headlines of Fleet Street. To understand its grip on the public imagination, one must examine the potent blend of an evocative setting, enduring mythological archetypes, the burgeoning power of mass media, and the very human drama played out by its central figures.

The primary stage for this drama, Highgate Cemetery, was almost a character in itself. By the late 1960s, this Victorian necropolis, with its magnificent but decaying gothic architecture, overgrown pathways, and shadowed catacombs, exuded an atmosphere thick with romantic desolation and inherent eeriness. Its state of neglect made it both a compellingly spooky locale and physically accessible for clandestine activities, whether real or imagined. Such a place naturally invites speculation and becomes a canvas upon which fears and fantasies can be readily projected. The crumbling angels and ivy-clad tombs provided the perfect, almost pre-scripted backdrop for a gothic horror story to play out in the real world.

The choice of a "vampire" as the antagonist was pivotal. The vampire archetype, deeply embedded in Western culture through folklore and, significantly, through literary works like Bram Stoker's Dracula, carries immense symbolic weight. It embodies ancient fears of death, the unknown, predatory evil, and forbidden sexuality. By the 1960s and 70s, amplified by decades of cinema, the vampire was an instantly recognizable and potent figure of horror. Seán Manchester's specific identification of the Highgate entity as a "King Vampire of the Undead" from aristocratic, Eastern European origins tapped directly into this rich vein of established mythology, lending the local scare an immediate and dramatic gravitas that David Farrant's initial, more ambiguous "grey figure" lacked in terms of sensational appeal.

The role of the media in escalating the Highgate Vampire story cannot be overstated. Local newspapers, particularly the Hampstead & Highgate Express, initially reported the strange occurrences, but it was the national tabloids and television news segments that propelled the narrative into a full-blown panic. The visual medium of television, showcasing interviews with Farrant and Manchester (often filmed on location in the cemetery), brought the story directly into people's homes with an immediacy that print alone could not achieve. The media not only reported the events but actively shaped them, focusing on the most sensational aspects, highlighting the rivalry between the two occultists, and giving platform to the most dramatic claims. This created a feedback loop: media coverage fueled public fear and interest, which in turn generated more stories and more coverage, a hallmark of a developing moral panic.

The personalities and public rivalry of David Farrant and Seán Manchester were central to the legend's development. Each man cultivated a distinct public persona and offered competing narratives and solutions to the alleged supernatural threat. Their accusations against each other, their claims of psychic battles and secret rituals, provided ongoing drama that kept the story in the public eye long after initial interest might have waned. This human element, the clash of self-styled vampire hunters, transformed the affair from a simple ghost story into a protracted public spectacle.

The socio-cultural context of the late 1960s and early 1970s also played a part. This was a period of significant social change, a *questioning of traditional norms, and for some, a burgeoning interest in occultism, mysticism, and alternative spiritualities as part of the wider counter-culture. While this doesn't explain the core events, it may have contributed to a public atmosphere more receptive to, or at least intrigued by, tales of the supernatural encroaching upon the mundane. The idea of ancient evils surfacing in modern London resonated with a time of uncertainty and flux.*

The phenomenon of the mass "vampire hunt" on March 13th, 1970, is a stark illustration of collective behaviour under the influence of fear and suggestion. It demonstrated how readily a group of people, primed by media narratives and a sense of imminent danger, could suspend disbelief and engage in actions that, viewed in retrospect, seem almost medieval. The image of hundreds of individuals, armed with makeshift stakes, converging on a cemetery in a major modern city is a powerful testament to the latent power of ancient fears.

Ultimately, the Highgate Vampire legend illustrates how a combination of factors – an evocative location, a potent mythological figure, intense media speculation, charismatic (and conflicting) personalities, and underlying societal anxieties – can coalesce to create an enduring modern myth. While the immediate hysteria has long since passed, and Highgate Cemetery is now carefully managed and preserved, the story of its alleged undead resident continues to fascinate. It serves as a cautionary tale about the power of suggestion and the ease with which fear can be manufactured and spread, but also as a testament to the enduring human fascination with the dark, the mysterious, and the things that go bump in the night, even in the most seemingly rational of times. The question of what really happened at Highgate may never be fully answered, and it is in this ambiguity that the legend retains much of its chilling power.

Black Shuck

Imagine the coast of East Anglia, a landscape scraped bare by the relentless winds off the North Sea. Picture the fens, vast and flat, where the sky feels too large and the horizon stretches into an unnerving infinity. Walk, if you dare, the ancient trackways that crisscross this land, paths worn smooth by centuries of feet, leading from one isolated hamlet to another through whispering reedbeds and across desolate heaths. It is here, in these lonely, liminal spaces, where the veil between worlds seems thinnest, that Old Shuck walks.

They call him by many names: the Black Dog of Bungay, the Hateful Thing, Old Shock, or simply Shuck. The name itself, some say, derives from an old word for "demon" or "shaggy," and shaggy he is often described. But it is his size that first seizes the breath – enormous, as big as a calf or a small pony, a creature of impossible dimensions. His coat is a matted, impenetrable black, the colour of a starless night or a fresh grave. And his eyes... ah, his eyes. Sometimes it is a single, cyclopean orb burning in the centre of his massive head, a malevolent lantern glowing with an infernal red, green, or yellow light. Other times, two saucer-sized pools of fire glare out from the darkness, fixing upon the unwary traveller with an intelligence that is anything but animal.

To meet Black Shuck on a lonely road as the light fails is an experience that sears itself into the soul. He often appears suddenly, without a sound. One moment, you are alone, the silence broken only by the cry of a distant curlew or the sigh of the wind through the marram grass. The next, he is there, padding silently beside you or blocking your path, a colossal silhouette against the fading twilight. No growl precedes him, no bark, no rustle of disturbed undergrowth. His passage is as spectral as the mists that often wreath these low-lying lands.

The air around him grows cold, a damp, grave-chill that settles deep in the bones, quite different from the natural bite of the coastal wind. A sense of profound dread descends, a primal fear that constricts the chest and quickens the pulse to a frantic drum. Some say a sulphurous odour accompanies him, the faint, acrid scent of brimstone. Others speak of his breath, visible as a spectral vapour even on a mild night, carrying a charnel house coldness.

He rarely attacks, not in the physical sense. His terror is more insidious, more psychological. He is an omen, a portent of doom. To see him is to know that death, for you or for someone close, is not far behind. He might pace you for a while, a silent, terrifying companion, his great head level with your shoulder. Or he might simply stand, barring your way, those terrible eyes burning into yours, stripping away all courage, leaving you hollowed out with a fear that has no name. Then, as suddenly as he appeared, he will be gone, vanishing into the gloom or passing through a solid gate or wall as if it were no more substantial than mist.

The lone walker, the late-night traveller, the fisherman heading home along the shingle beach – these are his chosen witnesses. They are left trembling, their skin clammy, their minds reeling from the encounter. And they carry the certainty of that unspoken warning. For weeks, months, sometimes years, they live with the shadow of that meeting, waiting for the inevitable. Because Black Shuck does not lie. His appearance is a promise, a dark covenant sealed by the sight of those damnable, glowing eyes. He is the essence of the fear that walks abroad in the lonely, forgotten places of East Anglia, a reminder that some ancient things still hold sway when the lights of modernity are far, far away.

The year is 1577. The month, a sweltering August. For centuries, Black Shuck had been a whisper on the wind, a fleeting terror on lonely roads, a dread omen spoken of in hushed tones. But on Sunday, the fourth day of that oppressive month, the beast would etch its passage not just into memory, but into the very stone and timber of God's own houses, leaving behind a scar of terror that time would not erase.

A storm gathered that morning, a monstrous, bruise-coloured congregation of clouds that clawed its way in from the grey expanse of the North Sea. It was no ordinary summer tempest. This was a thing of savage, almost sentient fury. The sky over Suffolk grew unnaturally dark, an apocalyptic twilight at midday. Rain lashed down in blinding sheets, and the wind howled like a tormented soul, ripping at thatch and rattling ancient window frames. Then came the thunder, not as distinct claps, but as a continuous, deafening bombardment, as if the heavens themselves were being torn asunder. And the lightning – that was the worst. It split the gloom with incessant, violent flashes, each one illuminating a world convulsed in terror.

In the small village of Blythburgh, nestled near the coast, the congregation of Holy Trinity Church huddled together, their prayers drowned out by the elemental chaos raging outside. The air within the ancient church grew thick with fear, heavy with the smell of damp wool and human apprehension. Suddenly, amidst a particularly deafening cannonade of thunder, the great wooden doors at the west end of the church burst inward with a sound like a musket shot.

For a heart-stopping moment, framed against the flickering, storm-wracked sky, stood a colossal black hound. It was Shuck, more terrible than any whispered tale had ever conveyed. His eyes, they said later, burned like hellfire, twin coals of damnation in the gloom. He was wreathed in an unnatural energy, lightning seeming to crackle around his massive form.

Before the stunned congregation could even draw breath to scream, the beast was among them. It moved with preternatural speed, a blur of black fur and malevolent purpose. It ran down the aisle, its claws scrabbling on the stone flags, a sound that would echo in nightmares for years to come. As it passed between two parishioners kneeling in terrified prayer, a man and a boy, it struck them down. They fell without a cry, their necks snapped, their bodies convulsing briefly before lying still. Others were seared by the demonic heat that radiated from the creature. The church steeple itself was struck by lightning that same instant, a great beam crashing down, as if heaven and hell were locked in furious combat.

Then, as quickly as it had entered, the demon dog was gone,

leaving behind it a scene of horror – the dead, the injured, the air thick with the smell of ozone and something else, something fouler. And upon the ancient oak door, scorched deep into the wood, were great black claw marks, the Devil's own fingerprints, a lasting testament to its blasphemous intrusion.

The storm, and Shuck, were not yet done. Some seven miles away, in the market town of Bungay, a similar terror was unfolding at St Mary's Church. The congregation there too was gathered for morning service, seeking solace from the raging tempest. Again, the thunder roared, a cacophony that seemed to shake the very foundations of the church. And again, amidst a blinding flash of lightning that plunged the interior into a momentary, terrifying darkness, the beast appeared.

It materialised within the church itself, some said between the terrified worshippers, a monstrous black shape with eyes like burning embers. It rampaged through the sacred space, its passage marked by chaos and death. Two men were killed instantly, struck down as they prayed, their bodies contorted in agony. Another man was grievously injured, shrivelled and burned as if by infernal fire, though he would survive to tell the tale, his skin forever marked by the encounter.

The chronicles of Abraham Fleming, writing shortly after these events, tell of the panic, the screams, the sheer, unadulterated terror of those trapped within the churches with this diabolical hound. He described it as "the devil in such a likeness," a creature of pure malice. When it finally vanished from Bungay, it too left its mark – scorch marks on the north door, another indelible sign of its passage.

That terrible Sunday, August 4th, 1577, burned itself into the collective memory of East Anglia. Black Shuck was no longer just a fleeting shadow on a lonely path. He was a proven terror, a demonic force capable of invading the most sacred of spaces, leaving death and destruction in his wake. The scorch marks on the doors of Blythburgh and Bungay churches can still be seen today, mute, chilling witnesses to the day the Devil's dog came to church. And the fear, the deep, visceral fear of that monstrous black hound, became a legacy passed down through the blood, a shadow that would forever haunt the Suffolk landscape.

The terrible storm of 1577 eventually blew itself out, leaving behind a ravaged landscape and communities reeling in shock and grief. The scorch marks on the church doors at Blythburgh and Bungay remained, stark and undeniable, but Black Shuck himself, the demonic hound that had brought such terror, melted back into the mists and shadows from whence he came. Yet, he did not truly depart. His presence lingered, a permanent stain on the psyche of East Anglia, a fear woven into the very fabric of the land and its people.

Through the centuries that followed, the tale of that dreadful Sunday was told and retold, whispered by firesides on stormy nights, recounted by grandparents to wide-eyed children. It became a cornerstone of local lore, a chilling reminder of the dark forces that could erupt into the ordinary world. And as the story was passed down, so too was the belief that Shuck still walked. The great dog was not a singular apparition, confined to one terrifying historical moment; he was an enduring entity, a phantom of the lonely roads and desolate coasts.

Sightings, though perhaps less dramatically documented than the church invasions, continued. Generation after generation, folk in Suffolk, Norfolk, and the Essex marshlands would speak of encounters with the great black hound. A farmhand, late returning from the fields, would see those burning eyes staring at him from the hedgerow. A fisherman, mending his nets by the shore as dusk fell, would feel the sudden, unnatural chill and turn to see the colossal silhouette padding silently along the shingle. A carriage driver, urging his horses along a dark, tree-lined lane, would find them suddenly rearing in terror, their eyes wide with a fear he could not initially comprehend, until he too saw the massive, dark shape that glided, rather than ran, beside them.

The interpretations of Shuck's nature, while rooted in the demonic terror of 1577, sometimes acquired nuances. To most, he remained an omen of death, his appearance a sure sign that someone in the community, or the unfortunate witness themselves, was marked. If his paw prints were found leading to a particular cottage, the inhabitants would brace themselves for a coming bereavement. But occasionally, a different kind of tale would surface. Some whispered that Shuck might, very rarely, act as a protector, guiding lost travellers safely through the fens, or guarding a lonely woman from harm, his terrifying presence ironically warding off more human threats. These tales, however, were exceptions, whispers against the prevailing wind of dread. For the most part, to meet Shuck was to brush against your own mortality, to feel the cold breath of the grave.

His appearance, too, remained largely consistent – the immense size, the shaggy black fur, the eyes like burning coals. Sometimes he was said to be headless, a truly grotesque variation, or to drag a spectral chain behind him, its clanking an unearthly sound in the stillness of the night. His silence, the utter lack of any sound accompanying his passage, remained one of his most terrifying attributes. He was a phantom, a creature not entirely of this world, moving through it yet not truly part of it.

Even into the 20th and 21st centuries, as the old ways faded and the landscape changed, as roads were paved and electric lights pushed back the darkness in towns and villages, the shadow of Black Shuck has never entirely receded. You can still find people in East Anglia who will speak of him with a hushed conviction, who will tell you of a relative's encounter, or a strange, unsettling experience of their own on a lonely stretch of coast or a quiet country lane after dark. The specific fear of a demonic dog may have softened for some into a more generalized unease about certain places, certain nights, but the legend endures.

He has become more than just a story; he is an atmosphere, an intrinsic part of the region's identity. Black Shuck is the wildness that can never be fully tamed, the ancient dread that lingers in the face of modernity. He is the shiver down your spine when you walk alone as night falls across the salt marshes, the sudden, inexplicable feeling of being watched from the shadows of an old churchyard. He is the lingering question: what if the old tales are true? What if, out there in the darkness, on those winding, forgotten paths, the great black hound still walks, its fiery eyes searching, its silent paws carrying it through the endless night? The terror of 1577 may be history, but the shadow of Black Shuck, it seems, is eternal.

Cultural Insights

The legend of Black Shuck, the monstrous spectral hound said to haunt the lonely roads, coastal paths, and churchyards of East Anglia, is one of the most potent and enduring folkloric traditions in the British Isles. More than just a simple ghost story, Shuck is a complex figure whose roots delve deep into the ancient fears, beliefs, and very landscape of the region. Understanding this entity requires looking beyond the chilling encounters to the cultural and historical soil from which it sprang.

Black Shuck is perhaps the most famous regional variant of a widespread archetype: the phantom black dog. Tales of enormous, dark hounds with glowing eyes are found throughout Britain – from the Barghest of Yorkshire and the North, often a portent of death or misfortune, to the Gytrash of Lancashire, which could be either benevolent or malevolent, and numerous other local spectral canines. These creatures often share core characteristics: their large size, shaggy black fur, luminous (often single) eyes, silent movement, and association with ancient trackways, crossroads, graveyards, or sites of violent death. They are frequently seen as omens, most commonly of death, but their meaning can vary. Shuck, particularly in his East Anglian manifestation, leans heavily towards the terrifying and doom-laden.

The name "Shuck" itself is suggestive. Most scholars trace it to the Old English word scucca (or sceocca), meaning "demon," "devil," or "fiend." This linguistic link immediately places the creature in a sinister, preternatural category. Alternatively, some suggest it may derive from a local dialect word meaning "shaggy" or "hairy," reflecting its common description. The demonic connotation, however, seems most resonant with the core mythology, especially following the events of 1577.

The origins of black dog lore likely predate Christianity. Some folklorists suggest these figures could be survivals of ancient guardian spirits, perhaps psychopomps (guides of souls to the afterlife) from Celtic or Germanic traditions. There are also plausible connections to Norse mythology, which had a strong influence in East Anglia during the Danelaw period. Odin, the Allfather, was often depicted accompanied by two wolves, Geri and Freki. It's conceivable that these divine companions, or other similar figures, could have morphed in the popular imagination over centuries into the more solitary and menacing figure of Black Shuck. The association of such creatures with storms, as seen in the

1577 accounts, also echoes the wild hunt motifs found in Germanic and Norse folklore, where a spectral huntsman and his hounds presage calamity.

The unique landscape of East Anglia – the flat, exposed fens, the often misty and desolate coastlines, the ancient Icknield Way and other old trackways – provides a perfect, atmospheric breeding ground for such a legend. These are liminal spaces, where the boundaries between the known and unknown can feel blurred, especially at night or in poor weather. The vast, open skies and the low-lying land can create optical illusions, and the region's historical isolation may have helped preserve older beliefs. Shuck is, in many ways, the genius loci of these lonely places, a spectral embodiment of their inherent wildness and mystery.

The events of August 4th, 1577, at the churches of Blythburgh and Bungay, are pivotal in the Black Shuck canon. Documented by the Reverend Abraham Fleming in Holinshed's Chronicles (1587 edition), these accounts provide a rare historical anchor for what might otherwise be considered purely folkloric. Fleming's vivid description of a "black dog, or the divel in such a likenesse," appearing during a terrifying thunderstorm, killing and injuring parishioners, and leaving scorch marks on the church doors, cemented Shuck's reputation as a demonic entity of immense power and malevolence. These were not fleeting glimpses on a dark road; these were invasions of sacred spaces, acts of terror witnessed by entire congregations. The physical "evidence" of the scorch marks, still pointed out today, lends a powerful verisimilitude to the tale.

Symbolically, Black Shuck can be interpreted in several ways. Most commonly, he is a death omen. His appearance foretells a demise, either for the witness or someone known to them. His association with storms in the 1577 incidents also aligns him with *natural destructive forces, perhaps even seen as a manifestation of divine wrath or demonic power unleashed. The silence of his passage, despite his great size, adds to his otherworldly, ghostly nature, while his fiery eyes are a classic attribute of infernal beings. While some black dog legends elsewhere in Britain occasionally depict the creature as a guardian of treasure or a protector of lonely travellers, this aspect is far less prominent in the core East Anglian Shuck tradition, which overwhelmingly emphasizes his terrifying and portentous nature.*

The psychological impact of such a legend is profound. It taps into primal fears: fear of the dark, of being alone in desolate places, of sudden, inexplicable death, and of the supernatural. The figure of a monstrous black dog is a potent symbol that can embody these anxieties. The persistence of Shuck sightings, even into the modern era, speaks to the enduring power of such archetypal fears and the human tendency to interpret unsettling experiences through the lens of existing folklore.

Black Shuck remains a living piece of East Anglian heritage. His image has appeared in local iconography, literature, and even music, most famously perhaps in the name of the rock band The Darkness, who hail from Suffolk and whose debut album featured a track titled "Black Shuck." The legend continues to fascinate and to chill, a reminder that some corners of the land retain their ancient mysteries, and that the spectral hound, whether a figment of folklore or something more, still casts a long, dark shadow over the imagination.

The Vanishing Hitchhiker of Blue Bell Hill

There's a stretch of the A229 in Kent, a ribbon of tarmac that snakes its way over the chalky spine of the North Downs, known as Blue Bell Hill. By day, it's just another busy road, thrumming with the mundane passage of commuters and lorries. But as twilight bleeds into night, and the traffic thins to a lonely trickle, Blue Bell Hill can take on a different character. The woods that crowd its verges seem to press closer, their branches like skeletal fingers. The wind, sweeping across the exposed heights, can whisper strange laments. And for those who know the stories, a particular section of this road, near the Lower Bell pub, carries a palpable weight, a chill that has little to do with the ambient temperature.

This chill, many believe, has its heart in a night of unimaginable tragedy. November 19th, 1965. The date is etched into the local memory. It was a Friday, dark and damp. Four young women, their lives vibrant and full of promise, were travelling home from a late shift. One of them, Judith Richardson, was a bride-to-be, her wedding day just a few short weeks away, her mind likely filled with dreams of white lace and happy futures. On that treacherous stretch of Blue Bell Hill, their car, a Ford Cortina, spun out of control in the gloom. The collision was catastrophic.

Three of the young women, including Judith, were killed instantly, their bright futures extinguished in a brutal moment of twisted metal and shattered glass. The fourth survived, but was gravely injured, a lone witness to a horror that would haunt her days. The news sent a shockwave through the local community, a wave of grief for lives cut so terribly, so senselessly short.

In the weeks, months, and years that followed, as the initial shock subsided, something else began to take root. Strange stories. Unsettling whispers. Drivers began to report unnerving experiences on that same stretch of road, particularly on dark, wet nights, nights much like the one that had claimed Judith Richardson and her friends. A feeling of profound sadness, an inexplicable coldness, would sometimes grip them as they passed the spot. Some would catch a fleeting glimpse of something at the edge of their headlights, something that vanished before it could be properly seen.

The road itself, already a place of sorrow, seemed to retain an echo of that night's tragedy. The air grew heavy with more than just the scent of damp earth and exhaust fumes; it carried a faint, almost imperceptible perfume of grief, a sense that something, or someone, had been left behind, unable to complete their journey. The ordinary asphalt, worn by countless tyres, seemed to weep a silent, invisible tear for the lives so violently interrupted. And it was from this sorrow, from this lingering echo of a shattered dream, that the spectral figure began to emerge, a lonely silhouette against the darkness, waiting patiently by the weeping stretch of road.

It might be a Tuesday night, or a Thursday, deep in the chill of late autumn, perhaps even on an anniversary close to that fateful November evening. Rain, that fine, persistent Kentish drizzle that seems to soak right through to the bone, slicks the tarmac of the A229. Headlights cut a lonely swathe through the darkness, the windscreen wipers beating a metronomic, almost hypnotic rhythm. You're a driver, perhaps James or Sarah, just an ordinary person heading home after a long day, or maybe making a late delivery. Your mind is on mundane things: the warmth of your house, a hot cup of tea, the day's lingering frustrations.

Then, as you navigate the familiar curves of Blue Bell Hill, near the dip by the Lower Bell, your headlights pick out a figure. Standing by the roadside, just beyond the ragged edge of the verge, is a young woman. She's alone, motionless, her form indistinct in the rain-streaked gloom. Your first thought is of concern, mixed with a flicker of apprehension. It's a desolate spot to be waiting, especially on a night like this. No broken-down car in sight, no other sign of life.

You slow down, your tyres hissing on the wet road. As you draw closer, you can make out more details. She's young, perhaps in her early twenties. Her clothes seem a little... out of place, not quite modern, though it's hard to tell in the poor light. Her face is pale, her expression unreadable, perhaps etched with a profound sadness. She doesn't wave or signal, just stands there, a solitary, rain-soaked sentinel.

Against your better judgment, perhaps, or spurred by a sense of duty, you pull over. The passenger door clicks open, a small invitation against the vast, indifferent night. "Need a lift, love?" you might ask, your voice sounding unnaturally loud in the confines of the car.

She doesn't say much, perhaps just a murmured "Thank you," or "To Chatham, if you're going that way." Her voice is quiet, almost a whisper, easily lost beneath the drumming of the rain on the car roof. She slides into the passenger seat, bringing with her a faint, inexplicable chill that makes the hairs on your arms prickle.

The journey continues in a strained silence. You try to make small talk, to fill the oppressive quiet. "Nasty night to be out," or "Bit late to be stranded, isn't it?" Her replies, if they come at all, are brief, monosyllabic. She stares straight ahead, her hands clasped in her lap. You might glance over, notice the pallor of her skin, the way her eyes seem fixed on some distant, unseen point. A strange unease begins to creep into your mind, a subtle disquiet that you can't quite name. The car heater hums, but that chill she brought in with her seems to linger, a pocket of cold air around her still form.

You drive on, perhaps for a few minutes, perhaps a mile or two. You might be in the middle of a sentence, pointing out a landmark or commenting on the weather again, when you turn to look at her.

And she's gone.

Just... gone. One moment she was there, a quiet, sorrowful presence beside you. The next, the passenger seat is empty. The seatbelt, if she'd worn one, is still buckled, undisturbed. The door is closed, locked as it was. There was no sound, no struggle, no indication that she had even moved. She has simply vanished, as if she were made of mist and rain.

Your heart hammers against your ribs. A cold sweat breaks out on your forehead. You might slam on the brakes, the car skidding slightly on the slick road, your eyes darting wildly around the empty interior, then to the dark, rain-lashed road behind you. Nothing. Just the empty night, the relentless drizzle, and the unnerving, echoing silence where your passenger had been.

Disbelief wars with a rising tide of terror. Did you imagine it? Were you dreaming? But the indentation on the passenger seat, the lingering faint chill, the undeniable memory of her quiet presence – these things scream that she was real. Or, at least, something was.

You sit there for a long moment, the engine idling, the wipers still clearing a view of nothing but the hostile night. Then, with trembling hands, you put the car back into gear and drive on, faster now, desperate to put miles between yourself and that haunted stretch of Blue Bell Hill. But the image of the pale girl, the chill she brought with her, and the utter impossibility of her disappearance – these things will ride with you, a silent, unwelcome passenger, for a very long time to come.

The vanishing passenger you encountered was not the first, nor would she be the last, to leave a bewildered driver trembling in the darkness of Blue Bell Hill. Yours is but one thread in a tapestry of similar tales, woven over decades, each encounter adding another layer to the chilling legend. For the spectral young woman, often believed to be the lingering spirit of Judith Richardson or one of her unfortunate friends, seems bound to that sorrowful stretch of road, her vigil unending.

Through the years, the reports have continued, a steady, unsettling drip of inexplicable encounters. Sometimes it is, as you experienced, the quiet girl who accepts a lift only to dematerialise. But her manifestations are not always so passive. Other drivers, their faces pale with remembered terror, have sworn they've seen a young woman dart suddenly into the path of their oncoming vehicle, a horrifying, spectral figure appearing from nowhere. They slam on their brakes, brace for the sickening impact, their hearts leaping into their throats... only to find nothing there. No crumpled body, no sign of an accident. Just the empty road, the thumping of their own pulse, and the chilling certainty of what they almost hit.

A frantic search of the verges reveals no one. Some drivers, shaken to their core, have called the police, reporting a terrible accident, a pedestrian struck. Investigations are launched, officers comb the area, but no victim is ever found, no report of a missing person matches. Only the unsettling consistency of these phantom near-misses, always on that same haunted incline.

Occasionally, the details shift. Some say the ghost is not always a hitchhiker but a solitary figure seen weeping by the roadside, her face buried in her hands, an image of inconsolable grief. Others have spoken of a different apparition, perhaps linked to another tragic accident that stained the A229 with sorrow in 1974, suggesting that Blue Bell Hill may be a place where multiple sorrows echo. But the most persistent, the most chilling, is the tale of the young woman, often thought to be a bride-to-be, her journey so tragically cut short, now seemingly forever trying to complete it, or perhaps to warn others of the dangers that lurk on that treacherous hill.

What does she want? That is the question that hangs in the

air after every encounter, as tangible as the morning mist that often clings to the Kentish downs. Is she searching for something she lost that terrible night – a locket, a dream, a future? Is she trying to convey a message, a warning from beyond the veil? Or is she simply an echo, a psychic imprint of profound trauma and sorrow, replaying her final moments, trapped in an endless loop of tragedy on that weeping stretch of asphalt?

No answers are ever forthcoming. The police files contain numerous reports of these strange occurrences, often logged with a weary sigh and a knowing glance between officers. Locals exchange stories in hushed tones, especially when the nights draw in and the rain falls on Blue Bell Hill. Some claim to know the exact spot where she appears, the particular tree or lay-by that marks her lonely station.

The legend has become a part of the hill itself, as ingrained as the chalk beneath the tarmac. It serves as a sombre reminder of life's fragility, of the way tragedy can sear itself into a place, leaving behind an echo that defies time and reason. And so, she waits. On dark nights, when the conditions mirror that long-ago November evening, the Vanishing Hitchhiker of Blue Bell Hill continues her silent, sorrowful vigil. And lone drivers still peer anxiously into the gloom, their hands tightening on the wheel, wondering if tonight, they too will offer a ride to a passenger in the dark, a passenger who will leave them with nothing but a chill in their soul and a story they will hesitate to tell, for fear of not being believed. But those who have seen her, they know. They know that some journeys never truly end.

Cultural Insights

The chilling tale of the Vanishing Hitchhiker of Blue Bell Hill is a powerful and remarkably persistent local legend in Kent, yet it also belongs to a much wider, almost universal, family of ghost stories.

Understanding this specific manifestation requires exploring not only its tragic local roots but also its connection to a deeply resonant folkloric archetype that has haunted lonely roads across the globe for generations.

At its core, the Blue Bell Hill story is a classic "Vanishing Hitchhiker" narrative. This archetype, documented in countless variations across numerous cultures, typically involves a driver picking up a lone traveller (often a young woman) on a desolate road, only for the passenger to inexplicably disappear from the moving vehicle. Often, the hitchhiker is later discovered to have been the ghost of someone who died tragically at or near that spot, sometimes even on an anniversary of their death. Variations include the ghost leaving behind an item (like a scarf or book), delivering a prophetic warning, or asking to be taken to a specific address which turns out to be their former home or grave. The Blue Bell Hill ghost primarily fits the sorrowful, lingering presence model, often linked directly to a known tragedy.

The most frequently cited origin for the Blue Bell Hill ghost is the horrific car accident that occurred on the A229 on the night of November 19th, 1965. Four young women were involved in a fatal collision near the Lower Bell pub. Judith Richardson, a 22-year-old bride-to-be, was killed along with two of her friends, Angela Morris and Patricia Krawczyk. A fourth friend, Yvonne Dennis, was seriously injured but survived. The profound local shock and grief following this event provided a potent emotional seed for a ghost story. The image of a young woman, her life and dreams of marriage so cruelly cut short, aligns perfectly with the archetype of the sorrowful female spirit often found in Vanishing Hitchhiker tales. While other fatal accidents have occurred on Blue Bell Hill over the years (including another in 1974 involving a runaway car that killed three people, sometimes also woven into the broader ghostly lore of the hill), the 1965 tragedy remains the most powerful anchor for the primary hitchhiking ghost.

The A229 road itself, particularly the stretch over Blue Bell Hill, plays a crucial role. It's a major route, historically a challenging one with steep gradients and sharp bends, though modern improvements have altered it significantly. Roads with a history of accidents often become focal points for such legends. The physical environment – the dark woods, the sometimes bleak and windswept nature of the North Downs, the isolation experienced by a lone driver at night – all contribute to an atmosphere conducive to eerie experiences and the perpetuation of ghost stories. The specific location of the sightings, often near the site of the 1965 crash, reinforces the connection to that tragedy.

Psychologically, such legends can be seen as expressions of collective grief, trauma, and the human need to make sense of sudden, tragic loss. The idea of a spirit "trapped" or "unfinished" due to a violent or untimely death is a common theme in ghostly folklore worldwide. The Vanishing Hitchhiker of Blue Bell Hill can be interpreted as an embodiment of unresolved sorrow, a psychic echo of that terrible night imprinted onto the landscape. For drivers who experience something inexplicable, the existing legend provides a framework for understanding their unsettling encounter.

The persistence of the Blue Bell Hill legend owes much to both oral tradition and media coverage. Local newspapers in Kent have periodically revisited the story, publishing eyewitness accounts and discussing the folklore surrounding the hill. Word-of-mouth, passed between drivers, locals, and paranormal enthusiasts, has kept the narrative alive and evolving. In more recent times, the internet has provided a new platform for sharing experiences and discussing the legend, ensuring its transmission to new generations. This demonstrates the resilience of such "road ghost" stories, even in an age of increasing skepticism.

The Blue Bell Hill Hitchhiker rarely seems malevolent; her appearances are more often tinged with sadness and a sense of gentle persistence. Unlike some road ghosts who are said to cause accidents or lure drivers to their doom, she is typically a passive, if profoundly unsettling, presence. The encounters often leave witnesses not just frightened, but also touched by a sense of pathos and mystery. This emotional resonance is key to the story's enduring power.

While the Vanishing Hitchhiker is a global phenomenon, the Blue Bell Hill version is a distinctly Kentish iteration, deeply rooted in a specific place and a known tragedy. It serves as a constant, albeit spectral, reminder of the fragility of life and the way that profound loss can become interwoven with the landscape itself, creating echoes that continue to haunt the living. The legend endures not just as a spooky tale, but as a poignant local memorial, a ghostly whisper on a dark and lonely road.

The Grey Lady of Hampton Court Palace

Hampton Court Palace. The name itself conjures a pageant of English history, a sprawling red-brick testament to ambition, love, betrayal, and the relentless march of time. Its vast courtyards, its echoing state apartments, its Tudor kitchens that once fed kings, and its manicured gardens that have witnessed centuries of royal secrets – all are steeped in a profound, almost tangible sense of the past. Walk its long, oak-panelled galleries, and you walk with ghosts, whether you believe in them or not. The very air seems thick with the sighs and whispers of those who lived, loved, and suffered within these imposing walls.

But beyond the grand narratives of monarchs like Henry VIII or William III, there are quieter echoes, more subtle hauntings that cling to the shadowed corners and less-trodden passages. Long before tour guides began to speak her name with a hushed reverence, staff members – the cleaners moving silently through the deserted state rooms at dawn, the security guards making their lonely rounds in the dead of night – would sometimes share unsettling experiences.

It might begin as nothing more than a sudden, inexplicable drop in temperature in a room that, moments before, had been comfortably warm. A localized chill, so intense it could raise gooseflesh, even on a summer's day, often felt in the apartments overlooking Clock Court or in the vicinity of what were once royal nurseries. Then there were the sounds. Faint at first, easily dismissed. A soft rustling, like the swish of a heavy silk gown, heard when no one was visibly present. A quiet sigh, seeming to emanate from an empty chair. The almost inaudible creak of a floorboard in a locked and vacant chamber.

Sometimes, it was the distinct, unnerving sensation of being watched. A feeling that would prickle at the back of the neck, causing one to turn sharply, only to find an empty corridor stretching away into the gloom, the portraits of long-dead courtiers the only silent witnesses. In these moments, the palace, for all its daytime grandeur, could feel profoundly lonely, profoundly ancient, and imbued with a subtle, pervasive sorrow.

These were not the dramatic clankings of chains or the terrifying apparitions that grace more violent ghost stories. This was something more nuanced, more melancholic. It was as if a gentle, sorrowful presence moved through the palace, unseen but keenly felt, a quiet guardian of forgotten moments, a silent watcher in the ancient halls. The identity of this presence was yet unknown to most, a whisper without a name, but the feeling she evoked was one of quiet sadness, of a duty perhaps unfulfilled, or a peace long disturbed. The grand tapestries and gilded ceilings bore witness to the comings and goings of kings and queens, but the very stones of Hampton Court seemed to hold the imprint of a quieter, more personal sorrow, waiting for its story to be fully heard.

For many years, the subtle disturbances within Hampton Court remained just that – unexplained whispers, fleeting chills, the sense of an unseen companion. But as the 19th century unfolded, events transpired that would seemingly give this sorrowful presence a name, a history, and a reason for her unquiet wanderings. The Grey Lady, as she would come to be known, is widely believed to be the spirit of Dame Sybil Penn.

Dame Penn was no queen or renowned noblewoman in the grand tapestry of Hampton Court's history, but her role was one of profound trust and intimate dedication. She was the beloved nurse to the young Prince Edward, son of the formidable Henry VIII and Jane Seymour. She tended to him with unwavering devotion, a steadfast presence in his young life, guiding him through childhood illnesses and offering comfort within the often-turbulent world of the Tudor court. When the dreaded smallpox swept through the household, striking the young prince, Sybil Penn nursed him tirelessly. Edward recovered, but Sybil herself tragically succumbed to the disease in 1562, her life given in service to her royal charge. She was laid to rest in the old church at Hampton, a village that lay in the shadow of the great palace she had served.

For nearly three centuries, Dame Sybil Penn rested in peace, her memory perhaps fading like the inscriptions on her tomb. But in 1829, progress, as it often does, came with a disregard for the slumber of the dead. The old church at Hampton, where Sybil Penn lay, was deemed dilapidated, and the decision was made to demolish it and build a new one. During this reconstruction, her tomb was disturbed, her earthly remains disinterred and moved.

It was shortly after this desecration, this unwelcome intrusion upon her eternal rest, that the phenomena at Hampton Court Palace began to change, to coalesce. The vague feelings of a presence sharpened into something more distinct. Occupants of certain apartments, particularly those in the southwestern wing which had historical connections to the royal nurseries or Sybil Penn's own lodgings, began to report a strange, persistent sound: the distinct, rhythmic whirring and clicking of a spinning wheel.

There was no spinning wheel in these rooms. Yet, the sound would come, often at dusk or in the quiet hours of the night, a ghostly echo of domestic industry, a sound intimately associated with the women's quarters of centuries past. It was a gentle sound, not frightening in itself, but deeply unsettling in its utter inexplicability. Who was this unseen spinner, her ghostly labours continuing beyond the veil of death?

Then came the sightings. A tall, slender figure, clad in a long grey gown, began to be seen moving silently through the corridors and chambers. She would appear suddenly, glide across a room, and then vanish, often through a closed door or into a solid wall. Her face was rarely seen clearly, often described as indistinct or shadowed by a hood or coif, but the overwhelming impression was one of profound sadness, of a gentle melancholy. She made no sound as she moved, offered no threat, simply passed through, a sorrowful echo of a life long ended.

The connection was made: the disturbed grave of Dame Sybil Penn, the loyal nurse, and this new, more defined spectral presence. It was believed that the disruption of her final resting place had disquieted her spirit, causing her to return to the palace where she had spent so much of her life, where she had dedicated herself to the care of her young prince. Perhaps she was searching for him, her maternal instincts reaching across the centuries. Perhaps she was simply seeking the peace that had been so rudely taken from her. The sound of the spinning wheel, some whispered, was her way of making her presence known, a familiar, comforting sound from her lifetime, now a poignant reminder of her unrest. The Grey Lady had found her name, and her sorrowful vigil within the ancient walls of Hampton Court had truly begun.

The centuries have turned, and Hampton Court Palace has transitioned from a seat of royal power to a magnificent historical treasure, its gates open to visitors from across the globe. Kings and queens no longer walk its halls as rulers, but as figures in a grand, unfolding history. Yet, Dame Sybil Penn, the Grey Lady, it is said, continues her quiet, sorrowful vigil, her presence an enduring whisper amidst the echoes of the past.

Her manifestations, though always subtle, have not ceased with the passage of time. Staff members, even in the bright light of the 21st century, still recount experiences that defy easy explanation. A security guard, making his rounds in the stillness of the State Apartments after the last tourist has departed, might feel that sudden, inexplicable drop in temperature in a specific corner of a gallery, a chill that raises the hairs on his arms despite the modern heating systems. Or a cleaner, working in the early hours before the palace awakens, might hear it – the faint, unmistakable whirring of a spinning wheel, seeming to come from just beyond a closed door, only to find the adjoining room empty, silent, and undisturbed.

Visitors, too, sometimes report fleeting encounters. A glimpse of a tall, grey-clad figure drifting silently at the end of a long corridor, mistaken for a costumed interpreter until she vanishes into thin air. An overwhelming sense of sadness, a profound and inexplicable melancholy, that might descend upon someone standing in Clock Court or near the old Tudor kitchens, a feeling so potent it brings tears to their eyes before lifting as suddenly as it came. Children, with their often unclouded perception, have occasionally pointed to an "empty" space and asked about the "sad lady in grey."

The areas most associated with her presence remain those linked to her life and her reputed earthly concerns. The apartments overlooking Clock Court, the vicinity of the historical royal nursery wing, and certain passages in the older, Tudor sections of the palace are where her subtle influence is most often felt. She does not scream, nor rattle chains, nor seek to terrify. Hers is a quieter haunting, more akin to a lingering sigh, a memory imprinted upon the very stones and timbers of the palace.

Why does she remain? That is the question that drifts through the ancient halls alongside her. Is she still searching for her young charge, Prince Edward, her devoted nurse's spirit unable to rest while he is lost to her in the mists of time? Is her peace still disturbed by the long-ago violation of her grave, her spirit forever unmoored? Or has she simply become a part of Hampton Court, an intrinsic element of its atmosphere, a keeper of its quieter sorrows, her essence interwoven with the countless other lives that have unfolded within its walls?

Perhaps there is no single answer. Perhaps she is all these

things. The Grey Lady of Hampton Court is not a figure of terror, but one of deep, abiding pathos. Her story is a poignant reminder that even within the grand theatre of history, amidst the clamour of kings and the fall of empires, it is often the quiet acts of devotion, the personal sorrows, and the gentle spirits that leave the most indelible, if spectral, mark.

So, if you walk the echoing corridors of Hampton Court, amidst the magnificent portraits and the priceless tapestries, listen carefully. Look closely. You might not see a king or queen from centuries past, but you might just feel a sudden chill, hear the faintest whisper of a spinning wheel, or catch a fleeting glimpse of a tall, sad figure in grey, still keeping her timeless, sorrowful watch. For Dame Sybil Penn, it seems, is a resident for eternity, a gentle phantom forever bound to the palace she served in life, and continues to grace, in her own ethereal way, in death.

Cultural Insights

The tale of the Grey Lady of Hampton Court Palace is a particularly resonant example of British ghostlore, blending historical figures, architectural grandeur, and the enduring human fascination with spirits tied to specific locations. Unlike more overtly terrifying apparitions, the Grey Lady embodies a quieter, more melancholic form of haunting, her story deeply entwined with themes of loyalty, disturbed rest, and the palpable weight of history that permeates the palace walls.

The "Grey Lady" is a common archetype in ghost stories across the British Isles and beyond. These spectral figures are typically female, often depicted in grey or muted attire (symbolic perhaps of mourning, indistinctness, or simply the pallor of a spirit), and are usually associated with a specific historic house, castle, or ruin. Their hauntings are frequently characterized by a sense of sadness, a lingering presence, or the replaying of a past sorrow or routine, rather than overt malevolence. The Grey Lady of Hampton Court fits this archetype beautifully, her legend rooted in a specific historical individual and a perceived injustice.

The ghost is widely identified as Dame Sybil Penn, the devoted nurse of Prince Edward, later King Edward VI, the son of Henry VIII. Historical records confirm Sybil Penn's existence and her service to the young prince, to whom she was deeply attached. She died of smallpox in 1562, an illness some versions of the legend claim she contracted from Edward himself after nursing him through it (though historical accounts of Edward VI's childhood illnesses are complex). Her burial in the old church at Hampton (then a village distinct from the palace grounds) is also a matter of record. This historical grounding lends a crucial layer of plausibility and poignancy to the ghost story, distinguishing it from more nebulous folkloric entities.

The commonly accepted catalyst for Dame Penn's spectral restlessness is the disturbance of her grave in 1829. During the demolition of the old Hampton church and the construction of the new St. Mary's Church, her remains were disinterred and, according to most accounts, moved or the memorial altered. This act of disturbing a final resting place is a powerful and ancient trope in ghostlore worldwide. It often signifies disrespect to the dead and is seen as a primary reason for a spirit's inability to find peace, leading to its return to familiar earthly haunts. The timing of increased ghostly reports at Hampton Court following this event is a cornerstone of the Grey Lady legend.

Hampton Court Palace itself is a veritable theatre of ghosts, its long and dramatic history making it a prime candidate for multiple hauntings. The tormented screams of Catherine Howard, Henry VIII's fifth wife, are said to echo in the gallery where she was dragged away to her doom. Henry VIII himself is sometimes reported as a brooding, intimidating presence. The Grey Lady fits into this spectral tapestry as one of its more gentle and persistent spirits. The sheer age of the building, its labyrinthine corridors, and the weight of human emotion – joy, sorrow, intrigue, and tragedy – that its walls have witnessed contribute to an atmosphere where the veil between past and present can feel exceptionally thin.

The specific manifestations attributed to Sybil Penn are rich in symbolism. The most famous is the sound of a spinning wheel, often heard in the apartments she is believed to have occupied or near the old royal nursery wing. Spinning was a common domestic activity for women of her era, associated with household duties, care, and quiet industry. For a nurse, it represents a comforting, almost maternal sound. Its ghostly persistence suggests a continuation of her caring duties, or perhaps simply an echo of her earthly life replaying itself. Her grey attire, as previously mentioned, is typical of the "Grey Lady" archetype, often signifying a sorrowful or unobtrusive spirit.

Unlike many spectral figures, Dame Penn's ghost is rarely described as frightening or malevolent. Instead, witnesses report feelings of sadness, inexplicable chills, or simply the calm, quiet presence of an unseen watcher. This aligns with her historical persona as a devoted caregiver. Her motivations for haunting are generally interpreted as either a search for her beloved royal charge, Prince Edward, or a sorrowful restlessness due to the disturbance of her earthly remains. She is often perceived as a benign, if sorrowful, "place memory" ghost – a spirit so intrinsically linked to a location and its emotional history that she has become part of its very fabric.

The legend of the Grey Lady continues to be a significant part of Hampton Court's visitor experience. It is recounted on ghost *tours, featured in books about the palace's history, and remains a subject of interest for paranormal investigators and enthusiasts. The story contributes to the palace's allure, adding a layer of romantic mystery to its historical grandeur. It highlights how folklore and genuine historical events can intertwine, creating narratives that resonate deeply with the human psyche – our respect for the dead, our fascination with the past, and our enduring curiosity about what might lie beyond the veil. The Grey Lady of Hampton Court is more than just a ghost; she is a poignant symbol of loyalty enduring beyond death, a quiet testament to the personal histories that whisper within the grand halls of power.*

The Enfield Poltergeist

Number 284 Green Street, Enfield, North London, was an utterly unremarkable council house. Semi-detached, pebble-dashed, it was just one of many identical homes lining a quiet suburban road. Inside lived Peggy Hodgson, a single mother doing her best to raise her four children: Margaret, thirteen; Janet, eleven; Johnny, ten; and Billy, seven. Their life in the late summer of 1977 was ordinary, filled with the usual routines of school, meals, and playtime, a life as unassuming as the house itself. But the thin veneer of that normality was about to be violently, inexplicably torn away.

It began subtly, as such things often do, with sounds that could almost be ignored, almost rationalized away. On the night of August 30th, Peggy was downstairs when young Janet and her younger brother Billy called out, complaining of noises in their shared bedroom. Billy, wide-eyed, spoke of his bed wobbling. Peggy, like any mother, probably sighed, expecting to find an overactive imagination or a loose floorboard. She went upstairs, checked under the beds, found nothing. "Settle down," she told them, "it's just the house settling."

But the next night, the sounds returned, more insistent this time. It started with a shuffling, like someone dragging their feet across the bare floorboards of the children's bedroom, even when the children themselves were tucked tightly into bed. Peggy listened, a knot of unease tightening in her stomach. This wasn't the usual creak and groan of an old house. This was different.

Then came the knocking. Four distinct raps on the party wall that separated their house from their neighbours, the Nottinghams. Peggy went next door. Had they heard anything? Had they knocked? Vic Nottingham, a burly builder, and his wife Peggy (coincidentally also named Peggy) had heard nothing, knocked on nothing. Baffled, Peggy Hodgson returned to her own home, the unanswered knocks echoing in her mind.

The focus of these early disturbances seemed to be Janet and Margaret's bedroom. The girls, particularly Janet, seemed more attuned to it, or perhaps more targeted by it. One evening, as Peggy was trying to settle them, a heavy chest of drawers in their room began to move. Not a slight tremor, not a gentle shift. It slid, scraping loudly across the floor, a good foot and a half away from the wall, all on its own.

Peggy stared, her heart hammering. She pushed it back, her muscles straining against its weight. It was a solid piece of furniture, not easily moved. As soon as she let go, it slid out again, with the same horrifying, deliberate motion. This was no loose floorboard. This was no childish prank. A cold dread, sharp and sickening, washed over her. This was something impossible, something wrong.

Panic began to set in. Peggy gathered her terrified children and fled next door to the Nottinghams, her face pale, her voice trembling as she recounted what she had seen. Vic Nottingham, a practical, no-nonsense man, was sceptical but agreed to investigate. He went into the Hodgson house, casting his eyes around the children's bedroom, searching for wires, for any trick. He heard the knocking himself then, sharp and distinct, seeming to come from the walls, from the ceiling, from nowhere and everywhere at once. He searched, he listened, he found nothing. But he left that house a deeply unsettled man, the easy scepticism wiped from his face. Whatever was happening at 284 Green Street, it was beyond his understanding. The ordinary house was no longer ordinary. Something had begun to stir within its unassuming walls, and the shuffling in the night was only the first, quiet breath of a gathering storm.

The moving chest of drawers was a horrifying turning point. What had begun as unsettling noises in the night now declared itself as a physical, tangible force within the Hodgson home. The flimsy reassurances Peggy had offered her children, and perhaps herself, were torn away. Sleep became a fraught, shallow affair, every creak of the house, every unexplained sound, now a potential prelude to some new terror. And the house at 284 Green Street did not disappoint. It seemed to awaken, flexing unseen muscles, its malevolence growing bolder with each passing day.

The knocking continued, louder now, more insistent, sometimes seeming to follow them from room to room, a mocking, invisible percussionist. But soon, it was joined by a barrage of other phenomena. Small objects – marbles, Lego bricks, coins – would suddenly take flight, whizzing across rooms as if thrown by an unseen hand, sometimes striking family members with surprising force. One evening, a heavy armchair in the living room spun around on its own and then crashed onto its side. Cushions would leap from sofas; drawers would fly open, their contents spewed across the floor.

The children's bedroom remained the epicentre. Janet, in particular, seemed to be a focal point for the entity's attention. She and Margaret would scream in the night, claiming unseen hands were pulling off their blankets, or that they were being forcibly pushed and pulled. Peggy would rush in to find them pale and trembling, their beds in disarray. On several occasions, Janet was allegedly thrown clean out of her bed, landing with a heavy thud on the floor, a small, terrified heap in the darkness. There were reports of her levitating, hovering briefly in the air, her nightgowned figure held aloft by an invisible power before being dropped unceremoniously.

The family's terror was acute. Peggy, a pragmatic woman by nature, found herself utterly out of her depth, her home transformed into a battleground against an enemy she could neither see nor comprehend. She was exhausted, frayed, desperate to protect her children who were bearing the brunt of this invisible assault. The ordinary comforts of home – a warm bed, a quiet room – became sources of dread. Every shadow seemed to lengthen, to take on a menacing form.

Neighbours, including the initially sceptical Vic Nottingham, witnessed some of these events firsthand. They saw objects move, heard the inexplicable crashes and bangs, and felt the unnatural cold spots that would suddenly appear and disappear in certain rooms. Their bewildered testimony added weight to

Peggy's increasingly desperate pleas for help.

Peggy called the police on more than one occasion. Officers arrived, expecting to find intruders or evidence of a prank. Instead, they too witnessed inexplicable events. One policewoman, WPC Carolyn Heeps, later signed an affidavit confirming she had seen a chair rise from the floor and move across the room unaided. But the police, for all their authority, were powerless. This was no ordinary crime, no human perpetrator they could apprehend. They could offer sympathy, suggest social services, but they could not stop the unseen tormentor.

The local vicar was called. He blessed the house, offered prayers, but the disturbances continued unabated, almost as if mocking his efforts. Peggy felt increasingly isolated, her sanity stretched to breaking point. The national newspapers, alerted by the growing local buzz, began to sniff around, intrigued by the sensational stories emerging from the ordinary council house.

Then, in early September 1977, a new figure entered the chaotic scene: Maurice Grosse, a member of the Society for Psychical Research (SPR). Grosse, an inventor by trade, had a deep personal interest in paranormal phenomena, an interest sharpened by his own recent family tragedy. He arrived at Green Street with his tape recorder and his open mind, prepared to investigate, to document, to try and understand the forces that had turned the Hodgson family's life into a waking nightmare. His arrival marked a shift. The family was no longer entirely alone with their terror. But the entity in their house, far from being cowed by this new scrutiny, seemed almost to relish the attention, preparing to unleash even more disturbing and direct manifestations of its presence. The house had awakened, and it was not yet done playing its terrifying games.

Maurice Grosse's arrival brought a measure of methodical observation to the chaos at 284 Green Street, but the entity, or entities, plaguing the Hodgson family seemed undeterred, perhaps even emboldened by the new audience. The flying objects, the knocking, the moving furniture – these physical manifestations continued their reign of domestic terror. But then, a new, deeply unsettling phenomenon began, one that would etch itself into the core of the Enfield legend and send a fresh wave of shivers down the spines of all who witnessed it. A voice began to speak.

It was not a disembodied voice, floating in the air. It seemed, almost impossibly, to emanate from young Janet Hodgson herself. Yet, it was utterly unlike her own childish tones. This was a rough, guttural growl, a rasping, masculine sound that seemed far too deep and gravelly to originate from the throat of an eleven-year-old girl. It was the voice of an old man, coarse and often angry, laced with profanities that made Peggy Hodgson blush and then tremble.

At first, it was just disjointed sounds, coughs and barks. But soon, words formed, then sentences. The voice would erupt from Janet, sometimes when she appeared to be in a trance-like state, her face contorted, her body seemingly a mere vessel for this unseen speaker. It claimed to be various entities, but one name emerged with chilling clarity: Bill Wilkins.

"Just before I died, I went blind," the harsh voice would croak, seemingly through Janet's lips, "and then I had a 'aemorrhage and I fell asleep and I died in the chair in the corner downstairs."

This "Bill Wilkins" claimed to have lived, and died, in the house years before the Hodgsons moved in. He spoke of his life, his family, his death. His pronouncements were often belligerent, filled with expletives, and punctuated by wheezing coughs that sounded ancient and diseased. He seemed to delight in tormenting the family and the investigators, swearing at them, threatening them, his words painting a picture of a bitter, earthbound spirit.

Maurice Grosse, armed with his tape recorder, spent hours in painstaking, often frustrating, dialogue with this entity. He would ask questions, and "Bill" would reply, his voice a shocking, rasping sound in the small council house rooms. The recorded tapes became a crucial, if controversial, part of the evidence, capturing these bizarre exchanges for posterity. Other voices sometimes manifested through Janet too – some childish, some seemingly female, adding layers of confusion and deepening the mystery. But it was "Bill" who became the dominant persona, the poltergeist's gruff, foul-mouthed spokesman.

The strain on Janet was immense. To have this alien voice seemingly usurp her own vocal cords, to be the conduit for such unsettling communications, was a terrifying ordeal. Sometimes she would appear exhausted, dazed after these episodes, with little or no memory of what "Bill" had said or done through her.

Around this time, another investigator from the Society for Psychical Research, Guy Lyon Playfair, joined Grosse. Playfair, an experienced researcher and author, brought a fresh perspective and further methodological rigour to the case. He too witnessed the voice phenomenon, marveling at its depth and apparent independence from Janet's conscious control, though he, like Grosse, remained acutely aware of the possibility of trickery, a suspicion that would hang over the case throughout its duration.

The emergence of the voice transformed the haunting. It was no longer just a series of physical disturbances; it now had a personality, a name, a history, however spectral and disputed. It suggested an intelligence, a conscious entity actively engaging with, and tormenting, the living. The ordinary house on Green Street had found its tongue, and the words it spoke were those of the dead, a chilling dialogue that echoed from beyond the veil, turning the Hodgson home into an arena for a truly unearthly conversation. The question of who, or what, was truly speaking remained a terrifying, unanswered riddle.

With the arrival of "Bill Wilkins's" spectral voice, the terrors at 284 Green Street seemed to reach a fever pitch, as if the entity, having found its means of communication, was now determined to demonstrate the full, frightening scope of its power. The Hodgson family, along with Maurice Grosse and Guy Lyon Playfair, found themselves under siege, not just from an unseen tormentor, but increasingly from a world that oscillated wildly between morbid fascination and outright disbelief.

The physical manifestations escalated beyond thrown objects and overturned furniture into more alarming and seemingly impossible events. Janet, still the apparent epicentre of the poltergeist's focus, was witnessed on several occasions being violently contorted or levitating. Photographs, now iconic in the annals of paranormal investigation, captured her mid-air, her body rigid, her face a mask of either terror or some strange, trance-like state. These moments were terrifyingly unpredictable; she might be sitting calmly one minute, only to be inexplicably lifted and thrown across the room the next, landing heavily, bruised but often, miraculously, not seriously injured.

Small, unexplained fires began to break out spontaneously. A tea towel might suddenly smoulder and burst into flames in the kitchen; a patch of carpet would scorch for no discernible reason. These incidents, though quickly extinguished, added a new, potentially lethal dimension to the haunting, forcing the family and investigators into a state of constant vigilance. The very air in the house often felt oppressive, charged with a malevolent energy. Objects didn't just fly; they sometimes bent or shattered in mid-air, as if twisted by an invisible, powerful hand.

Life for the Hodgsons became an unbearable ordeal. Sleep offered no escape, as nights were often punctuated by bangs, crashes, and Janet's tormented cries or the guttural pronouncements of "Bill." The children were exhausted, their schooling disrupted, their young lives consumed by fear and the relentless, bewildering phenomena. Peggy Hodgson, worn down by sleeplessness and the constant strain of protecting her family while trying to maintain some semblance of normality, was pushed to the edge of her endurance. The ordinary council house had become a prison, its walls echoing not with family laughter, but with the sounds of an unseen war.

The intense media attention that the case attracted was a double-edged sword. While it brought offers of help and a sense that they were not entirely alone in their struggle, it also invited a harsh glare of scrutiny and widespread scepticism. Accusations began to surface that the children, particularly Janet, were faking the phenomena. She was a bright, perhaps mischievous girl, and some observers suggested she was a gifted ventriloquist, expertly throwing the "Bill" voice, or that she and Margaret were orchestrating the moving objects through cleverly concealed tricks.

Video footage captured by a television crew, seemingly showing Janet bending spoons and attempting to hide a tape recorder, fueled these doubts, providing ammunition for those who believed the entire affair was an elaborate hoax. The investigators themselves, Grosse and Playfair, were acutely aware of these suspicions. They documented instances where they felt the children might have been embellishing or even faking certain events, particularly when they felt they weren't being given enough attention or when the "real" phenomena had temporarily subsided. This ambiguity became a hallmark of the Enfield case – moments of seemingly undeniable, inexplicable paranormal activity existing alongside incidents that raised serious questions.

The house on Green Street became a paranormal crucible, a place where belief and doubt clashed fiercely. Investigators tried to maintain objectivity, meticulously logging events, setting up cameras, and attempting to create controlled conditions, but the poltergeist, if that's what it was, seemed to defy easy categorization, operating by its own capricious rules. The family, already tormented by the entity, now faced the added pressure of public disbelief and accusations of fraud. They were trapped, caught between a terrifying, unseen force and a world that struggled to comprehend, let alone believe, their nightmarish reality. The siege was total, both from within their haunted walls and from the sceptical world outside.

Like a violent storm that eventually exhausts its fury, the relentless barrage of paranormal activity at 284 Green Street began, slowly and almost imperceptibly at first, to subside. There was no dramatic final confrontation, no definitive exorcism that banished the entity once and for all. Instead, over a period extending into 1979, the flying objects became less frequent, the guttural pronouncements of "Bill Wilkins" faded into longer and longer stretches of silence, and the terrifying levitations and physical assaults on Janet seemed to cease. The unseen tormentor, for reasons known only to itself, appeared to be withdrawing, its energy waning, or perhaps its purpose, whatever it might have been, fulfilled.

For the Hodgson family, the gradual quieting of their haunted home was met not with immediate relief, but with a kind of wary, exhausted disbelief. Had it truly gone? Or was this merely a lull, a cruel trick before some new onslaught? They had lived under siege for so long, their nerves frayed, their sense of security shattered, that the return to anything resembling normality was a slow and difficult process. The house on Green Street, though physically intact, would forever be marked by the invisible scars of those terrifying two years. The children, particularly Janet, who had borne the brunt of the entity's focus and the world's intrusive scrutiny, carried the psychological weight of their ordeal long after the last unexplained knock had faded. Their childhood had been stolen, replaced by a bewildering and terrifying chapter that set them apart, leaving an indelible mark on their lives.

The Enfield Poltergeist case, however, did not fade quietly into obscurity. It remains one of A most thoroughly documented, and fiercely debated, cases in the history of psychical research. The sheer volume of recorded evidence – audiotapes of the voice, photographs of alleged levitations and moving objects, numerous eyewitness testimonies from neighbours, police officers, journalists, and the investigators themselves – ensured its enduring notoriety.

To believers, Enfield is a landmark case, providing compelling, if often disturbing, evidence of poltergeist activity and even intelligent, discarnate communication. They point to the phenomena witnessed by multiple, credible individuals, the specificity of "Bill Wilkins's" historical claims (some of which were later found to have a degree of factual basis), and the sheer impossibility of young children, however mischievous, faking the entirety of such prolonged and varied manifestations.

To sceptics, Enfield is a masterclass in juvenile trickery, amplified by credulous investigators and sensationalist media. They highlight the instances where Janet and Margaret were suspected, or even caught, attempting to fake phenomena. The controversial video footage, the times the "voice" only seemed to appear when Janet's face was obscured or her lips could not be clearly seen, all fuel the argument that it was an elaborate, attention-seeking hoax that spiralled out of control.

Perhaps the truth, as is often the case in such complex and emotionally charged situations, lies somewhere in the murky grey area between these two extremes. Could it have begun with genuine, inexplicable phenomena, later embellished or augmented by the children, consciously or unconsciously, under the immense pressure of the situation and the constant demand for "activity" from investigators and the media? Did a troubled adolescent girl, perhaps unknowingly, become the focal point for genuine psychokinetic energy, while also resorting to trickery when that energy waned or when she felt overwhelmed?

These questions remain, hanging heavy and unanswered over the legacy of 284 Green Street. The house itself, after the Hodgsons eventually moved on, has been occupied by other families, who have reported little to no unusual activity, suggesting that the phenomena were indeed tied to the Hodgsons, particularly Janet, as is often theorized in poltergeist cases.

The Enfield Poltergeist has left an undeniable impact on popular culture, inspiring numerous books, documentaries, and feature films, each attempting to capture the terror and ambiguity of those disturbing years. It serves as a stark reminder of how an ordinary family, in an ordinary home, can find themselves at the epicentre of events that defy rational explanation, pushing the boundaries of our understanding of the world and the forces that may, just may, exist beyond our everyday perception.

An uneasy silence eventually fell upon Green Street, but the echoes of the knocking, the flying objects, and the rasping voice of "Bill" continue to resonate. The Enfield Poltergeist remains a chilling enigma, a story that refuses to provide easy answers, leaving behind a legacy of profound unease and the unsettling knowledge that sometimes, the most terrifying horrors are those that unfold within the familiar walls we call home.

Cultural Insights

The Enfield Poltergeist case, which unfolded in a modest council house in North London between 1977 and 1979, remains one of the most heavily documented, intensely scrutinized, and fiercely debated episodes in the history of psychical research. Its enduring notoriety stems not only from the extraordinary range of reported phenomena but also from the complex interplay of human psychology, media sensationalism, and the persistent, unsettling questions it left in its wake.

The events at 284 Green Street largely fit the profile of a classic poltergeist disturbance. Such cases, whose name derives from the German for "noisy spirit," typically involve a range of physical manifestations: unexplained noises (raps, bangs, shuffling), moving objects (from small items being thrown to heavy furniture being overturned), and occasionally, physical assaults on individuals. Crucially, poltergeist activity is often, though not exclusively, centered around an adolescent, leading to theories that the phenomena may be an unconscious externalization of stress, emotional turmoil, or psychokinetic energy – the "human agent" theory. Eleven-year-old Janet Hodgson was quickly identified as the apparent focal point of the Enfield disturbances.

The late 1970s in Britain provided a fertile ground for such a story to capture public attention. While the initial wave of counter-cultural interest in the occult from the late 60s had somewhat matured, there was still a significant public appetite for the paranormal, fueled by books, documentaries, and a press often eager for sensational content. The Enfield case, with its ordinary setting and extraordinary claims, quickly became a media phenomenon, extensively covered by newspapers like the Daily Mirror and even garnering television news attention, which brought the family's plight, and the investigators' efforts, into homes across the nation.

The primary investigators, Maurice Grosse and Guy Lyon Playfair, both members of the Society for Psychical Research (SPR), played a pivotal role in documenting the case. Grosse, driven by a personal interest in the paranormal, was the first on the scene and remained deeply involved throughout. Playfair, an experienced journalist and researcher, brought a more critical, though still open-minded, approach. Their extensive tape recordings, photographs, and detailed logs form the backbone of the Enfield archive. Their presence, however, also became part of the controversy, with sceptics suggesting they may have inadvertently influenced events or become overly invested in a paranormal interpretation.

Perhaps the most distinctive and contentious aspect of the Enfield case was the emergence of the deep, guttural "voice" seemingly emanating from Janet, claiming to be, among others, "Bill Wilkins," a man who had supposedly died in the house. This vocal phenomenon, captured on numerous audiotapes, shifted the case beyond typical poltergeist activity (often considered mindless or elemental) towards something suggesting an intelligent, discarnate entity. Attempts were made to verify Bill Wilkins's story, with some success in corroborating details about his death, adding another layer of intrigue. However, the voice itself was also a major focus for accusations of fraud, with suggestions that Janet was using ventriloquism or sophisticated trickery.

The debate over hoax versus genuine phenomena raged throughout the investigation and continues to this day. Sceptics point to instances where the children, particularly Janet and her older sister Margaret, were suspected or even caught attempting to fake events – bending spoons, hiding a tape recorder, or making noises when they believed they were unobserved. Even Playfair, in his book on the case, "This House is Haunted," acknowledged that the children were not always truthful and sometimes engaged in pranks, which he attributed to a desire for attention or a way of coping with the immense pressure.

Conversely, proponents of a paranormal explanation highlight the sheer volume and variety of phenomena witnessed by multiple individuals, including police officers, neighbours, and journalists, who had no prior investment in a supernatural interpretation. Events like furniture moving on its own in front of several witnesses, unexplained fires, and Janet's alleged levitations (famously photographed, though the images themselves are also debated) are cited as difficult to explain through trickery alone. The consistency of certain phenomena over a long period, despite intense scrutiny, also lent weight to the argument for a genuine underlying paranormal cause.

The psychological dimensions of the case are profound. The Hodgson family, particularly Peggy and her children, endured immense stress, living in a constant state of fear and unpredictability, their home invaded not only by the alleged entity but also by a stream of investigators, journalists, and curious onlookers. *The pressure of being the centre of such a sensational story, coupled with the accusations of hoaxing, undoubtedly took a heavy toll. Theories exploring adolescent stress as a trigger for psychokinetic outbursts were, and remain, prominent in attempts to understand the case.*

The Enfield Poltergeist left an indelible mark on paranormal lore. It is often cited as one of the most compelling, if problematic, poltergeist cases on record. Its influence can be seen in numerous books, documentaries, and fictional portrayals, most notably the film The Conjuring 2, which brought a dramatized version of the events to a global audience.

Ultimately, the Enfield Poltergeist remains an unsettling enigma. It offers no easy answers, instead presenting a complex tapestry of inexplicable events, human fallibility, intense psychological pressure, and the persistent ambiguity that often characterizes investigations into the paranormal. Whether a genuine haunting, an elaborate hoax, or a complex interplay of both, the events at 284 Green Street serve as a potent reminder of the mysteries that can erupt within the most ordinary of settings, challenging our perceptions of reality and the hidden forces that may lie just beyond our understanding.

The Loch Ness Monster

Loch Ness. The name itself rolls off the tongue with a sense of deep time and deeper mystery. It is a colossal gash in the Scottish Highlands, a twenty-three-mile-long, fiercely deep chasm filled with water so cold, so dark with suspended peat, that sunlight penetrates but a few scant feet below its often-turbulent surface. Its depths plunge to over seven hundred and fifty feet, deeper than much of the North Sea, creating a vast, hidden kingdom, an underwater realm largely unseen and unknown by the world above. The sheer volume of water it holds is staggering, more than all the lakes in England and Wales combined. This is no mere pond; it is an inland sea, an abyss cradled by brooding mountains and ancient forests.

For centuries, whispers have emanated from its shores, carried on the Highland winds. Tales of water horses, kelpies, and other strange, elusive creatures inhabiting its Stygian waters were woven into the fabric of local Gaelic folklore. These were the old stories, the fireside warnings, the personifications of the loch's often treacherous nature and its profound, unknowable depths.

The earliest recorded encounter that hints at something more tangible, something monstrous, dates back to the 6th century. Adamnán, in his Life of St. Columba, recounts how the Irish monk, while near the River Ness which flows from the loch, came upon locals burying a man who had been savaged by a "water beast." Undeterred, Columba ordered one of his followers to swim across the river. As the man did so, the beast, with a mighty roar and open jaws, surfaced and made towards him. Columba, witnessing this from the bank, raised his hand, made the sign of the cross, and commanded the creature in a thunderous voice, "Go no further! Do not touch the man! Go back at once!" And the beast, it is said, "fled terror-stricken in swift retreat, as if dragged by ropes," much to the astonishment of both the monks and the pagan Picts who witnessed the miracle.

For centuries after Columba's encounter, the monster, if it was indeed the same, remained largely the preserve of local legend, a shadowy inhabitant of a remote and sparsely populated region. But then came the 1930s, and the world began to change around Loch Ness. A new road, the A82, was blasted along its western shore, offering unprecedented views of the loch's surface to passing motorists. Suddenly, more eyes than ever before were gazing out over that vast expanse of dark water.

And the water, it seemed, began to gaze back.

In April 1933, a local couple, Mr. and Mrs. Aldie Mackay, were driving along this new road when Mrs. Mackay looked out at the usually placid loch and saw an "enormous animal rolling and plunging on the surface." Her husband stopped the car, and they watched, transfixed, as this "whale-like fish" or "monster," as they later described it, churned the water into a frenzy before disappearing beneath the waves. Their account, reported in the Inverness Courier by its correspondent Alex Campbell (who first used the word "monster" in print), ignited a spark.

Just a few months later, in July of that same year, George Spicer and his wife had an even more startling encounter. As they drove near the loch, they saw an "extraordinary form of animal" with a long, undulating neck, some twenty-five feet in length, lumbering across the road in front of their car, heading towards the loch, carrying what appeared to be a lamb or similar small animal in its mouth. They described its body as "Loch Ness, July 1933. About 4pm. It was a most extraordinary form of animal... hideous... an abomination." Their terror and conviction were palpable.

These sightings, and others that quickly followed, were different from the ancient myths. They were modern encounters, reported by ordinary people in broad daylight. The press seized upon the stories. "Monster of Loch Ness!" screamed the headlines. The quiet, brooding loch had awakened, and the world was suddenly desperate to know the secret hidden within its dark, peat-stained heart.

The initial flurry of sightings in 1933 acted like a flare sent up from the dark waters of Loch Ness, illuminating a mystery that the world found irresistible. The hunt was on. Amateur sleuths, dedicated researchers, curious tourists, and hard-nosed journalists all began to converge on the loch's shores, their eyes scanning the inscrutable surface, hoping for a glimpse of the creature that had so suddenly, so dramatically, surfaced from the realm of ancient myth into modern headlines. This was the golden age of Nessie hunting, a period marked by tantalizing "evidence," fervent expeditions, and an almost obsessive global fascination.

In April 1934, the image that would define the Loch Ness Monster for decades appeared. Published in the Daily Mail, the "Surgeon's Photograph," purportedly taken by Lieutenant Colonel Robert Kenneth Wilson, showed a long, serpentine neck and small head rising gracefully from the dark water. It was a stunning, almost elegant depiction of a plesiosaur-like creature, the quintessential image of a prehistoric survivor hidden in the loch. The photograph caused an international sensation. Here, it seemed, was irrefutable proof. Sceptics pointed to inconsistencies, to the convenient anonymity of Wilson (who claimed he didn't want his name associated with it initially), but for many, this was the evidence they craved. The image became iconic, reproduced countless times, cementing the long-necked image of Nessie in the public consciousness.

The loch itself became a theatre of watchful waiting. Sir Edward Mountain, in that same year of 1934, funded an extensive expedition, employing a team of twenty men equipped with cameras and binoculars to keep a constant vigil over the water for five weeks. They logged several fleeting sightings, brief disturbances on the surface, but no definitive photograph or capture. The monster, it seemed, was as elusive as it was intriguing.

Through the 1940s and 50s, despite the intervening war years, the reports continued – boatmen, local residents, and visitors alike would recount their own brief, often startling, encounters with an unidentified presence in the loch. Then, in

1960, another piece of compelling visual evidence emerged. Aeronautical engineer Tim Dinsdale, on a solo expedition, captured several feet of grainy 16mm film showing a large, dark hump moving across the surface of the loch, leaving a V-shaped wake, before submerging. The Dinsdale film, unlike the static Surgeon's Photograph, showed movement, purpose. It was analysed by RAF photographic experts who deemed it to be an animate object of considerable size, not easily explained away as a boat or floating debris. Dinsdale's footage reignited serious interest and spurred a new wave of investigation.

Organisations like the Loch Ness Investigation Bureau (LNIB), later the Loch Ness and Morar Project, were formed, bringing a more systematic, if often underfunded, approach to the search. They deployed mobile camera units, sonar equipment, and even, in later years, small submarines, all attempting to pierce the loch's murky veil. Sonar contacts were made on numerous occasions – large, moving objects detected in the depths that defied easy identification as known fish or geological features. Sometimes these contacts would seem to approach the sonar beams, then shy away, adding to the tantalising sense of an intelligent, wary creature navigating its hidden domain.

The chase for this shadow in the deep was filled with moments of high excitement and crushing disappointment. A promising sonar trace would turn out to be a thermal layer in the water or a shoal of salmon. A compelling photograph would later be exposed as a hoax or a misidentification of a deer swimming, an otter, or even a string of ducks. The infamous Surgeon's Photograph itself, decades later, would be revealed as an elaborate prank involving a toy submarine and a sculpted head.

Yet, despite the hoaxes, the misidentifications, and the lack of a definitive biological specimen, the core mystery endured. Too many credible, sober individuals had reported seeing something inexplicable. The Dinsdale film, though debated, remained a compelling piece of footage. The sonar contacts, while not conclusive proof of a monster, hinted at large, unknown objects moving with purpose in the abyss. The hunters kept watching, their gaze fixed on the dark, peat-stained water, fueled by the conviction that beneath that inscrutable surface lay one of the world's greatest zoological mysteries, a secret that the loch guarded jealously, offering only fleeting, maddening glimpses of the marvel, or the monster, that lurked within.

The fervent chase for Nessie, with its tantalizing photographs, grainy films, and mysterious sonar blips, inevitably collided with the cool, dispassionate gaze of scientific scrutiny. As the decades wore on, and no definitive biological specimen – no carcass washed ashore, no bone fragment dredged from the depths, no unambiguous DNA from a large, unknown creature – emerged, the chorus of scepticism grew louder. Zoologists pointed to the inherent unlikelihood of a breeding population of large, air-breathing reptiles surviving undetected in the cold, nutrient-poor waters of Loch Ness. Where was their food source? How did they avoid more frequent, undeniable sightings? The very idea of a relic from the age of dinosaurs, a living plesiosaur, seemed increasingly a romantic fantasy rather than a biological probability.

Alternative explanations for the sightings were proposed, each attempting to strip away the layers of mystery and offer a more mundane reality. Could the long necks and humps be misidentified known animals? A line of swimming otters, their heads and backs breaking the surface in sequence, could certainly mimic an undulating form. A deer swimming across the loch, its head and antlers held high, might appear strange and unfamiliar to an unsuspecting observer from a distance. Large fish, like sturgeon (though not native, occasional wanderers have been suggested) or exceptionally oversized eels, were also put forward as candidates.

Natural phenomena, too, offered plausible alternatives. The loch, due to its shape and the prevailing winds, is prone to unusual water disturbances. Wind slicks can create dark, moving patches on the surface that look deceptively like the back of a creature. Standing waves, or seiches, caused by oscillations of the entire body of water, can produce temporary humps and disturbances. Floating logs, mats of vegetation, or even the wake of a distant, unseen boat, especially when viewed through heat haze or in tricky light conditions, could all fool the eye.

And then there were the hoaxes. The stunning revelation in the 1990s that the iconic "Surgeon's Photograph" was an elaborate prank, a model monster attached to a toy submarine, dealt a significant blow to the credibility of some of the most compelling "evidence." This, coupled with other, less famous, admitted fakes, cast a long shadow of doubt over many other anomalous photographs and sightings.

Yet, despite the weight of scientific scepticism, the plausible alternative explanations, and the proven hoaxes, the mystery of the Loch Ness Monster refused to die. For every debunked photograph, there remained sincere, compelling eyewitness accounts from seemingly credible individuals who swore they had seen something inexplicable, something that did not fit neatly into any rational category. The Dinsdale film, though grainy and open to interpretation, continued to trouble the absolute sceptics. The sonar contacts, while not definitive proof of a monster, hinted at large, unidentified objects moving with purpose in the abyssal depths.

The loch itself seemed to conspire to keep its secrets. Its immense size, its Stygian, peat-stained waters that offer virtually zero visibility beyond a few feet, and its sheer, unfathomable depth make it an incredibly difficult environment to explore thoroughly. It is a place where something large could theoretically hide, a vast, dark, underwater wilderness. This very unknowability, this physical barrier to definitive proof or disproof, became the monster's greatest ally, allowing the legend to endure.

Even today, though the global media frenzy has long subsided, the watch continues. Webcams scan the surface, sophisticated sonar surveys are occasionally undertaken, and visitors still arrive at the loch's shores, their eyes hopefully scanning the dark waters. And still, the occasional, fleeting sighting is reported, a ripple on the water, a strange shape in the distance, just enough to keep the legend breathing.

Nessie has become more than just a potential undiscovered species; she is a cultural icon, a beloved enigma, a symbol of the enduring human fascination with the unknown and the desire for mystery in an increasingly mapped and rationalized world. Perhaps there is no single, giant creature patrolling the depths. Perhaps the "monster" is a complex tapestry woven from misidentification, folklore, human hope, and the profound, almost primal, atmosphere of Loch Ness itself.

Or perhaps, just perhaps, in that cold, dark, unfathomable abyss, something truly ancient and unknown still glides silently through the peat-stained gloom, its existence a secret whispered only to the deep water and the listening Highland winds. The loch keeps its counsel, and the mystery of its most famous resident remains, tantalizingly, just beyond our grasp.

Cultural Insights

The Loch Ness Monster, affectionately known as "Nessie," is arguably the world's most famous cryptid, a global icon of mystery whose legend transcends the murky waters of its Highland home. More than just a tale of an elusive creature, the story of Nessie is a complex interplay of ancient folklore, modern media, scientific inquiry, human psychology, and the profound allure of the unknown, all set against the backdrop of one of Scotland's most majestic and enigmatic lochs.

The notion of a strange beast inhabiting Loch Ness is not a purely 20th-century invention. The earliest recorded encounter dates back to the 6th century AD, detailed in St. Adamnán's Life of St. Columba. In this account, the Irish monk supposedly saved a man from a "water beast" in the River Ness (which flows from the loch) by making the sign of the cross and commanding the creature to retreat. While framed as a miracle, this tale indicates that local populations already held beliefs about a dangerous aquatic entity. Furthermore, Scottish folklore is rich with tales of water kelpies, water horses, and other mythical creatures said to inhabit lochs and rivers, often luring unwary travellers to a watery grave. These ancient traditions may have provided a fertile folkloric soil for the modern Nessie legend to take root.

The "monster boom" that ignited global fascination began in earnest in 1933. The construction of a new road (the A82) along the loch's western shore provided unprecedented views of the water's surface to a greater number of people. Key sightings, such as those by Aldie Mackay and George Spicer (who claimed to see the creature on land), were reported in the Inverness Courier, with journalist Alex Campbell famously using the word "monster." This media attention, particularly the publication of the "Surgeon's Photograph" in the Daily Mail in April 1934 – depicting a serpentine head and neck – catapulted Nessie to international stardom. Though later revealed as a hoax, this image profoundly shaped the public perception of the creature as a plesiosaur-like relic from a prehistoric age.

Loch Ness itself is a crucial element of the legend. It is the largest body of freshwater in Great Britain by volume, over 20 miles long, a mile wide, and plunging to depths of over 750 feet. Its waters are exceptionally murky due to high peat content from surrounding soils, severely limiting underwater visibility. Situated in the Great Glen, a massive geological fault line, the loch is deep, cold, and its ecosystem capable of supporting a substantial biomass, though whether enough to sustain a population of large predators remains a point of debate. These physical characteristics make it an ideal hiding place for a large, unknown creature and render definitive searches incredibly challenging.

Nessie is the quintessential subject of cryptozoology, the pseudoscience dedicated to searching for animals whose existence is unproven. The pursuit of Nessie has inspired countless expeditions, from amateur enthusiasts with binoculars to more organized efforts employing sonar, underwater cameras, and even small submarines (such as the operations by the Loch Ness Investigation Bureau). While these expeditions have produced intriguing sonar contacts and some ambiguous photographic or film evidence (like Tim Dinsdale's 1960 film), none have yielded irrefutable proof of a large, unknown animal species.

The scientific community remains largely sceptical, citing the lack of physical evidence (bones, carcasses, clear DNA), the biological implausibility of a prehistoric reptile surviving in such an environment, and the likelihood that sightings can be attributed to misidentification of known animals (eels, otters, deer, birds), natural phenomena (wind slicks, seiches, floating debris), or hoaxes. The impact of confirmed hoaxes, like the Surgeon's Photograph, has further fueled this scepticism.

Despite this, belief in Nessie, or at least a fascination with the possibility, endures. This persistence can be attributed to several psychological and sociological factors. There is an innate human desire for mystery, for the idea that the world still holds undiscovered wonders. "Expectant attention" can also play a role; visitors to Loch Ness, primed by the legend, may be more likely to interpret ambiguous stimuli as the monster. The legend provides a powerful "spirit of place," imbuing the beautiful but austere landscape with an added layer of enchantment and intrigue.

The economic and cultural impact of Nessie on the Loch Ness region and Scotland as a whole is undeniable. The monster is a major tourist draw, supporting a significant local industry of boat tours, visitor centres, and merchandise. Nessie has become a beloved, if elusive, national icon, instantly recognizable worldwide and featured in countless books, films, television shows, and popular culture.

In recent decades, the intensity of "monster hunting" has perhaps waned, but the allure remains. Modern technology, from advanced sonar to online webcams continuously monitoring the loch, has been employed, yet Nessie remains as elusive as ever. The story of the Loch Ness Monster is a testament to the power of legend, the deep human connection to place, and our enduring fascination with the unfathomed mysteries that may still lurk beneath the surface of our understanding, or indeed, beneath the dark, peat-stained waters of a Scottish loch.

The Screaming Skull of Bettiscombe Manor

Deep in the rolling countryside of Dorset, where ancient lanes twist between high hedgerows and time seems to move at a slower, more considered pace, stands Bettiscombe Manor. It is an old house, its stones weathered by centuries of wind and rain, its windows like dark eyes gazing out over fields that have seen countless seasons turn. Like many such manors, it holds its history close, its rooms steeped in the lives and deaths of generations who have passed within its walls. But Bettiscombe holds more than just the usual echoes of the past; it harbours a specific, tangible relic of a profound and terrible sorrow – a human skull.

For as long as anyone could clearly remember, the skull had been there. It rested not in a forgotten crypt or a sealed off chamber, but often in a more accessible, if still unsettling, place – perhaps on a dusty shelf in the attic, or tucked away in a seldom-used storeroom, sometimes even brought down to a more prominent, if still disquieting, position. It was discoloured with age, a fragile, ivory-to-yellowed dome of bone, its empty sockets staring out with a blind, accusing permanence.

It was not spoken of lightly. Children growing up in the manor learned of its presence in hushed whispers, their imaginations painting terrifying spectres around the stark reality of the human remnant. Servants would often avoid the room where it was kept, or hurry past its resting place with a quick, averted glance and perhaps a hastily muttered prayer. There was an unspoken understanding, a heavy, almost physical sense of unease that surrounded the skull. It was more than just bone; it was a sentinel, a silent watcher, imbued with a potent, dormant power.

Locals in the nearby village knew of it too. "The skull at Bettiscombe," they'd say, their voices dropping, a note of old fear and respect mingling in their tones. Stories circulated, as they always do around such objects – tales of strange noises in the night, of doors creaking open on their own, of an inexplicable coldness that would sometimes pervade the very air around the skull's resting place. These were dismissed by some as the products of an overactive imagination, the natural consequence of living with such a macabre relic.

But those who lived within the manor, those who felt its constant, silent scrutiny, knew it was more than that. They felt the weight of its story, even if the precise details had become blurred by time and retelling. They sensed the profound unhappiness tethered to those ancient bones, the echo of a terrible injustice, a broken promise that time had not healed. The skull was a fixture, an unyielding part of Bettiscombe's fabric, and though it often sat in silence, there was a terrifying potential held within its hollow gaze, a promise of unspeakable horror should its silent vigil ever be truly disturbed. The air around it was thick with this unspoken threat, a fragile peace maintained by a fearful respect for the unknown power it held.

The silent dread that permeated Bettiscombe Manor around its grim relic was rooted in a story of distant lands, human cruelty, and a solemn vow betrayed. Though the mists of time have clouded precise dates and names, the most enduring account whispers of the Pinney family, masters of Bettiscombe, who, like many landed gentry of their era, held plantations in the sun-scorched West Indies, their fortunes built upon the sweat and sorrow of enslaved people.

It is said that one Azariah Pinney, or perhaps another scion of the family, returned from Nevis or some such island bringing with him a black servant. This man, whose true name is lost to the winds of history, served his master faithfully, a displaced soul in the cool, damp climes of Dorset, far from the warmth of his homeland. He was loyal, diligent, and perhaps, in his heart, he carried a deep and abiding yearning for the place of his birth. As he lay dying – from illness, or old age, or simply a broken heart, the stories vary – he extracted a solemn promise from his master: that upon his death, his body, or at least his bones, would be returned to his native soil, to rest finally with his own people beneath the sun he remembered.

The master, perhaps moved by a moment of conscience or simply wishing to ease the passing of a faithful retainer, gave his word. The promise was made.

But promises, especially those made by the powerful to the

powerless, are fragile things. When the servant breathed his last, the practicalities and expense of transporting human remains across the vast ocean proved inconvenient. Or perhaps the vow was simply forgotten, dismissed as the dying fancy of a man whose life, in the eyes of his master, held little true consequence. Whatever the reason, the promise was broken. The servant's body was interred not in the warm earth of his distant home, but in the cold, alien soil of an English churchyard, some say at St. Stephen's Church in Bettiscombe village.

It was after this betrayal, after the earth had been piled upon his coffin, that the true terror began. Some say it started when the master, perhaps uneasy with the unfulfilled vow, or finding the grave a disquieting reminder, decided to have the skull exhumed and brought into the manor for some forgotten, macabre reason. Others claim the skull was separated and kept from the outset. Regardless of how it came to be a solitary relic within the house, the attempt to deny the servant his final wish, to sever his connection to his homeland, unleashed a fury that Bettiscombe Manor would never forget.

The first time an attempt was made to remove the skull from the house, or to bury it definitively where it did not belong, the very air seemed to split asunder. Bloodcurdling screams, inhuman in their intensity and filled with an agony that chilled the marrow, erupted from nowhere and everywhere at once. They filled the manor, echoed through its ancient corridors, and spilled out across the surrounding fields, terrifying livestock and striking dread into the hearts of anyone within earshot. These were not the cries of any living creature; they were the raw, amplified anguish of a tormented spirit, a soul denied its rest, its final plea for justice made hideously, terrifyingly audible.

The screams were just the beginning. Violent poltergeist

activity erupted. Doors slammed open and crashed shut with bone-jarring force, even when there was no wind. Windows shattered as if struck by unseen fists. Heavy furniture would scrape across floors, or be overturned. A palpable, malevolent presence filled the house, an icy rage that seemed to target the living with its fury. Some tales speak of sudden, violent storms that would whip up around the manor whenever the skull was disturbed, lashing the house with wind and rain as if nature itself were in league with the tormented spirit. Illness would strike the household, livestock would die inexplicably, and a pall of misfortune would descend upon all who resided within Bettiscombe's walls.

Terrified and bewildered, the Pinney family, or their descendants, made the connection. The disturbances, the screams, the ill fortune – it all stemmed from the skull, from the broken promise. In desperation, the skull was brought back into the manor, treated with a fearful respect it had previously been denied. And as it was restored to a place within the house, the screaming would subside, the violent activity would cease, and an uneasy, watchful peace would return. The lesson was learned, brutally and unforgettably: the skull demanded its place within Bettiscombe. It would not be buried where it did not belong, nor would it suffer removal. It was a prisoner, perhaps, but it was also a powerful, unyielding jailer, holding the entire household hostage to its eternal, screaming grief.

And so, an uneasy, chilling truce was struck between the living inhabitants of Bettiscombe Manor and the screaming skull that held dominion within its walls. The relic, once a symbol of a master's broken promise and a servant's stolen peace, became a fearsome fixture, a silent, bony tyrant whose unspoken rules were learned through terror and respected out of sheer, unadulterated dread. It was to remain within the house, unburied, undisturbed. To defy this edict was to invite a wrath that the stoutest heart could not endure.

Through the passing generations, as the Pinney family line continued or the manor passed to new hands, the skull remained. Its story was whispered from parent to child, from outgoing tenant to apprehensive newcomer. It sat, often tucked away in the attic or a quiet back room, a discoloured memento mori, a constant, palpable reminder of the power it wielded. For a time, perhaps for many years, it would be still, its presence merely a heavy weight on the atmosphere of the old house, a source of quiet unease rather than active terror.

But human nature is a curious thing. Scepticism blooms in times of peace. Newcomers, unbound by the ancestral fear, would arrive. Or perhaps a younger generation, raised on tales that seemed more folklore than fact, would decide to test the boundaries of the legend. Surely, they would think, in a more enlightened age, such a thing could not hold true. A mere skull, however tragic its origins, could not command the elements or fill a house with screams from beyond the grave.

And so, inevitably, attempts would be made. Someone, driven by a desire to give the remains a "proper Christian burial," or simply to be rid of the oppressive presence, would resolve to remove the skull from Bettiscombe. With determined, if perhaps trembling, hands, the skull would be taken from its accustomed place, carried from the manor, and interred in consecrated ground, or sometimes merely hidden away, thrown into a pond, or discarded in a field.

The results were invariably, terrifyingly, the same.

No sooner would the skull be separated from the manor, or its perceived sanctity violated, than the screaming would begin anew. Those bloodcurdling, disembodied wails would erupt, seeming to issue from the very stones of the house, from the earth beneath, from the air itself. They were screams of pure, unadulterated agony and rage, amplified by some unearthly power, capable of driving listeners to the brink of madness. The house would once again become a theatre of poltergeist fury. Doors would slam, objects would fly, and a chilling, malevolent presence would make itself known. Misfortune would once again plague the household and the estate. Sickness, accidents, inexplicable financial ruin – the skull's vengeance was varied and relentless.

Each time, the lesson was relearned with fresh terror. Chastened and horrified, the disturbers would retrieve the skull, often with considerable trepidation, and restore it to its place within Bettiscombe Manor. And, as before, upon its return, the screaming would cease, the disturbances would fade, and the oppressive, watchful silence would descend once more.

The skull, it became clear, was not merely a passive relic; it was an unyielding guardian of its own sorrow and its own strange domain. It had claimed Bettiscombe Manor as its prison, or perhaps its sanctuary, and it would not be moved. It demanded its presence be acknowledged, its strange, silent power respected.

Living with such an entity became a psychological burden, a constant, low hum of fear beneath the surface of daily life. Every unexplained creak of the floorboards, every sudden chill, every shadow in a dimly lit corridor could be attributed to the skull, a reminder of its watchful presence. It was a silent tenant, paying no rent, yet holding the ultimate lease on the peace of mind of all who dwelt there.

To this day, the Screaming Skull of Bettiscombe Manor is

said to remain, though the house has passed through various hands and its story continues to evolve with each telling. Scientific examinations have been made, suggesting the skull might be that of a prehistoric woman rather than a C17th male servant, adding another layer of mystery but doing little to dispel the core terror of the legend. For whatever its true origins, the power attributed to it, the sheer, unearthly horror of its screams as recounted through generations, has cemented its place as one of Britain's most chilling and enduring paranormal tales. It stands as a grim testament to the belief that some promises, once broken, can unleash a sorrow so profound, so powerful, that not even death can silence its cry. And at Bettiscombe, the silence itself is often the most terrifying sound of all, for it is a silence that listens, and waits.

Cultural Insights

The legend of the Screaming Skull of Bettiscombe Manor is a potent and deeply unsettling thread in the rich tapestry of British folklore. It belongs to a distinct sub-genre of supernatural tales centered on "screaming skulls" or other human remains that fiercely resist removal from a specific location, unleashing terrifying phenomena when disturbed. Understanding this particular skull requires delving into its historical context, its folkloric parallels, and the powerful themes of broken promises and spectral vengeance that animate its chilling story.

The motif of the "screaming skull" is not unique to Bettiscombe. Several other historic houses in Britain lay claim to similar unquiet relics. Wardley Hall in Lancashire, for instance, is home to a skull reputed to be that of a persecuted Catholic priest, which violently objects to any attempt to remove it. Burton Agnes Hall in Yorkshire has its own screaming skull, said to be that of Anne Griffith, who insisted her head remain in the house after her death. These tales share common elements: the skull is inextricably linked to a particular dwelling, attempts to bury it or take it away result in horrific screams and paranormal disturbances (poltergeist activity, storms, bad luck), and an uneasy truce is eventually established wherein the skull is left undisturbed, becoming a feared and respected fixture of the household. The Bettiscombe skull fits neatly into this eerie tradition.

The most widely accepted origin story for the Bettiscombe skull – that it belonged to a black servant or slave of a Pinney family member, brought from their West Indies sugar plantations – infuses the legend with a particularly dark historical resonance. The Pinney family of Dorset were indeed significantly involved in the Caribbean sugar trade and owned plantations on the island of Nevis from the late 17th century through to the abolition of slavery. This historical reality of colonial exploitation and the brutal system of enslavement lends a powerful, if deeply uncomfortable, verisimilitude to the tale of a wronged individual whose dying wish for repatriation was callously disregarded. The skull, in this context, becomes a potent symbol of historical injustice, its screams an eternal protest against the dehumanization and broken faith inherent in that system.

The folkloric power of a dying wish, especially the desire for proper burial in one's homeland, is immense. Across cultures, the belief that a spirit cannot find peace if its funeral rites are ignored or its body is not laid to rest in its rightful place is deeply ingrained. The betrayal of such a solemn vow to the Bettiscombe servant is presented as the primary catalyst for the curse. His spirit, denied the solace of ancestral earth, becomes tethered to the symbol of his earthly remains – his skull – and, by extension, to the home of the master who broke that sacred trust. The screams are the most visceral expression of this betrayal, an unending articulation of anguish, rage, and a desperate yearning for the peace he was denied.

The specific manifestations of the curse – the bloodcurdling screams, the violent storms that often accompany attempts to move the skull, the poltergeist activity within the manor, and the general misfortune that befalls those who defy it – are all classic expressions of a powerful, angered spirit. The screams themselves are the legend's most defining feature, a sound so terrible it transcends ordinary human experience, suggesting a supernatural origin. The storms link the skull's displeasure to the very elements, emphasizing its perceived power over the natural world surrounding the manor.

Living with such a legend, and indeed such a physical object, undoubtedly had a profound psychological impact on the inhabitants of Bettiscombe Manor. The constant awareness of the skull's presence, and the terrifying consequences of disturbing it, would create an atmosphere of perpetual, low-level dread. This fear, passed down through generations and reinforced by local tradition, would ensure the skull's continued "protection" and the perpetuation of its story. Each unexplained noise or misfortune could be attributed to the skull's displeasure, further solidifying its power in the minds of those who lived under its silent, watchful gaze.

Interestingly, attempts to scientifically examine the skull have yielded results that sometimes conflict with the most popular version of the legend. One notable examination suggested the skull was much older than the 17th or 18th-century setting of the Pinney/servant story, possibly belonging to a prehistoric female. However, such scientific findings often do little to dispel the power of a deeply entrenched folkloric narrative. The legend, with its compelling themes of injustice and supernatural retribution, has a life of its own, often proving more resilient than empirical data. Indeed, the mystery surrounding the skull's true origins may even add to its mystique.

The Screaming Skull of Bettiscombe Manor remains a potent legend, reflecting not only a fear of the restless dead but also, perhaps, a societal reckoning with historical wrongs. It speaks to the enduring belief that profound injustice can create an equally profound spiritual disturbance, one that echoes through centuries, demanding remembrance and respect. The skull, whether that of a betrayed servant or an ancient woman, stands as a chilling monitor of promises kept and the terrible consequences of disturbing those who should be at peace.

The Children of Woolpit

The sun of a long-ago August beat down upon the fields surrounding the small Suffolk village of Woolpit. It was the time of harvest, during the tumultuous reign of King Stephen, a period when England was often a harsh and uncertain land. But here, amidst the golden stalks of wheat and barley, the rhythm of life was dictated by the ancient pulse of the seasons. Men and women toiled under the summer sky, their sickles flashing, their voices calling out in the familiar cadences of medieval English. The air was thick with the scent of cut grain, dust, and honest sweat. It was a scene of earthy, predictable labour, a world grounded in the tangible realities of soil and sustenance.

Woolpit itself, a straggling collection of wattle-and-daub

cottages clustered around a simple church, drew its name from the deep, ancient pits dug nearby – wolf pits, designed in generations past to trap the predators that once roamed these lands. These pits, some long abandoned and overgrown, were places of shadow and local superstition, holes in the earth that children were warned to avoid.

On one such harvest day, as the reapers worked near the edge of these old excavations, a sound disturbed their labour. Not the familiar call of a bird or the rustle of wind, but something else, something that made them pause, their brows furrowed. It was a faint, distressed crying, thin and reedy, seemingly coming from the direction of the pits. Curiosity, perhaps tinged with a wary apprehension, drew a few of them closer.

What they found at the edge of one of the deeper wolf pits caused them to halt, their mouths agape, their sickles forgotten in their hands. Two small figures, a boy and a girl, huddled together at the pit's bottom, their faces streaked with tears, their bodies trembling. But it was not their distress alone that stunned the hardened field workers into silence. It was their skin.

The children were green. Not a sickly, jaundiced yellow-green, but a distinct, verdant hue, like the young leaves of an oak tree in spring, a colour utterly alien to human flesh. Their clothes, too, were strange, made of a coarse, unfamiliar fabric, cut in a style none of the villagers had ever seen. And when they spoke, their words were a cascade of strange, lilting syllables, a language that bore no resemblance to English, French, or any tongue known in that part of the world.

Fear mingled with profound bewilderment. Were these fey creatures, spirits of the wood or the earth itself? Or were they simply lost, albeit impossibly strange, children? The reapers, after a moment of stunned hesitation, driven by a basic human compassion that transcended their fear, carefully helped the pair from the pit.

The green children blinked in the bright Suffolk sunlight, their eyes wide and seemingly unaccustomed to such brilliance. They were small, of a delicate build, the girl slightly older than the boy. They clung to each other, their strange, green hands clasped tightly, their incomprehensible babbling filled with an evident terror and confusion. The villagers gathered around, a circle of ruddy, sun-browned faces staring in utter astonishment at these two impossible apparitions who had, quite literally, emerged from a hole in the earth. The ordinary harvest day had been shattered. Something utterly outside their understanding had stepped into their world, and the village of Woolpit would never be quite the same again.

News of the strange green children spread through Woolpit like wildfire, drawing curious and fearful onlookers. After much bewildered discussion, it was decided to take the pair to the nearby manor of Sir Richard de Calne, a knight of good standing, who, it was hoped, might offer them succour and perhaps unravel the mystery of their origin. Sir Richard, a man of his time, was no doubt as astonished as his tenants, but Christian charity, or perhaps a nobleman's curiosity, compelled him to take the children in.

Brought into the unfamiliar surroundings of Sir Richard's household, the green boy and girl remained utterly disconsolate. They wept continuously, their strange, musical cries echoing through the stone corridors, a sound that tugged at the hearts of even the most hardened servants, yet also unsettled them profoundly. Their green skin, in the flickering torchlight of the manor, seemed to glow with an even more unearthly luminescence. Their garments, made of that unknown, roughly textured material, were unlike anything seen in Christendom. And still, they babbled in their incomprehensible tongue, their words like the chattering of strange birds, conveying nothing but their deep distress and fear.

For several days, the children refused all sustenance. The cooks of the manor, puzzled but kind, offered them bread, meat, milk – the staples of an English diet. But the green children would turn away, their faces contorted in what seemed like revulsion or simply utter incomprehension. They grew weaker, their green pallor deepening, their cries becoming fainter. It was feared they would starve, these strange visitors from an unknown world.

Then, by chance, some freshly harvested beans – fabae, the broad beans or green beans common in English fields – were brought into the room where the children were kept. Upon seeing these, a flicker of recognition, of desperate hunger, ignited in their eyes. They gestured eagerly, their strange words taking on a new urgency. When the raw beanstalks were offered, they seized them, not breaking open the pods as the English did, but, according to some accounts, trying to open the hollow stalks themselves, weeping afresh when they found them empty. When shown how to open the pods, they fell upon the raw green beans within, devouring them with a desperate, almost animalistic hunger. For a long time, these beans were the only food they would touch.

The villagers and the household of Sir Richard de Calne watched them with a mixture of pity, awe, and trepidation. Who were these children who subsisted only on green things, whose skin matched the verdure they consumed? Where had they come from that they knew not bread nor meat? Attempts to communicate were met with blank incomprehension on both sides. Their language remained a beautiful, baffling stream of sound.

The boy, always the more delicate of the two, began to fade. Perhaps the unfamiliar diet, despite the beans, was not enough. Perhaps the shock of this bright, loud, alien world was too much for his young spirit. Or perhaps he simply yearned too deeply for the green-tinged land he had lost. He grew listless, his green skin taking on a duller, more sickly hue. His cries weakened. Despite the girl's frantic attempts to comfort him, to coax him to eat, he slipped away, dying quietly in that strange Suffolk manor, a small, green enigma to the last.

The girl, now utterly alone, her last link to her familiar world severed, was consumed by a profound grief. Her sorrow was a palpable thing in the household. Yet, with the resilience of youth, and perhaps out of sheer necessity, she slowly, tentatively, began to adapt. She started to sample other foods, and as her diet broadened, a remarkable change began to occur. The strange green tint of her skin began to lessen, gradually fading, over many months, to the more familiar pallor of an English maiden. She was still an object of immense curiosity, but the terrifying alienness was slowly receding, replaced by a poignant, solitary strangeness. And as her skin changed, so too did her tongue begin to loosen, as she started, haltingly, to learn the language of her captors, or keepers. The world waited to hear her story.

Left alone in a world that was not her own, the green girl of Woolpit, whose given name, Agnes, she would later adopt in baptism, slowly began to anchor herself to this strange, sunlit reality. The vibrant green of her skin, which had so astonished the Suffolk villagers, continued to fade as she gradually accepted the hearty English fare offered to her, the rich breads, meats, and pottages replacing the singular diet of raw beans. Over many months, her complexion softened to the hue of her human caretakers, leaving only a whisper of her former verdancy, a subtle, almost luminous pallor that still set her apart.

More remarkably, her tongue, once a fount of incomprehensible, lilting sounds, began to shape itself around the harsher, more guttural cadences of the English language. She was, by all accounts, intelligent and observant, and as the barriers of communication crumbled, the household of Sir Richard de Calne, and indeed all of Woolpit, waited with bated breath to hear her story. Where had she and her brother come from? What was the nature of the land that pigmented its people the colour of spring leaves?

And when she could finally articulate her memories, the tale she told was more wondrous and perplexing than any could have imagined.

She spoke, in her newly acquired English, of a place she called St. Martin's Land. It was, she said, a country that lay far beneath the earth, a realm where the sun as they knew it in Woolpit never shone. Instead, a perpetual twilight reigned, a soft, diffused green light that bathed everything in its ethereal glow. All the inhabitants of St. Martin's Land, she claimed, were green, just as she and her brother had been. They lived, she said, a Christian life, with churches and a semblance of order, though much of her description of their customs and way of life remained hazy, filtered through the lens of a child's memory and the difficulties of translating an alien experience into a new tongue.

She remembered a great river that separated their land from another, a "land of light," which they could sometimes glimpse across the waters, shining with an alluring, almost painful brightness.

One day, she recounted, she and her brother were tending their father's flocks in the fields – fields, one must imagine, that grew under that strange, subterranean twilight. They heard a wondrous sound, a clamour of bells, louder and more beautiful than any they had ever known. Drawn by this captivating melody, they wandered, following the sound into a great cavern or passage that burrowed through the earth. They walked for a long time, through darkness and echoing chambers, the sound of the bells luring them ever onward.

Suddenly, they emerged from the passage, blinking, into a dazzling, almost blinding light – the bright, unfamiliar sunshine of the English harvest fields. The sheer intensity of it, so different from their accustomed twilight, disoriented and terrified them. It was there, at the mouth of the wolf pit, that the reapers of Woolpit had found them, lost, afraid, and impossibly green, the sound of the village church bells still perhaps echoing in their ears. How they had travelled so far, or from what manner of place, she could not fully explain. She only knew that once they had emerged, they could not find the entrance to the passage again, their path back to St. Martin's Land lost to them forever.

Her story, when it was retold by the chroniclers of the age, such as Ralph of Coggeshall and William of Newburgh, was met with wonder, with piety, and with no small amount of scholarly debate. Was St. Martin's Land a real, subterranean world, a hidden faerie realm, or perhaps even some allegorical representation of another state of being? Or was it the confused, dream-like recollection of a traumatized child, her green skin the result of some strange malady or dietary deficiency (chlorosis, or "green sickness," was a known, if poorly understood, condition, though it rarely produced such a vibrant hue)?

Agnes, it is said, lived on in Woolpit for many years, eventually marrying a man from nearby King's Lynn. Some accounts describe her as "rather loose and wanton in her conduct," perhaps a lingering wildness from her strange origins, or simply the judgment of a medieval society on a woman who would always be an outsider.

The mystery of the Green Children of Woolpit has never been truly solved. Their tale remains suspended between folklore and historical account, a strange, poignant footnote in the annals of medieval England. Were they visitors from another dimension, lost faerie children, or simply human waifs whose origins were obscured by illness and cultural misunderstanding? The wolf pits of Suffolk have long since been filled in, but the enigma of the two small, green figures who emerged from them on that long-ago harvest day endures, a whisper of the uncanny in a world that often prefers its wonders to remain unexplained.

Cultural Insights

The strange and poignant tale of the Green Children of Woolpit stands as one of England's most captivating medieval mysteries, a curious blend of historical record and folkloric wonder that has intrigued scholars and storytellers for centuries. Unlike many legends that emerge from indistinct oral traditions, the appearance of these verdant youngsters is documented by two near-contemporary chroniclers, lending it a fascinating, if still perplexing, claim to reality.

The primary historical sources for the story are the accounts of Ralph of Coggeshall (died c. 1226), an abbot of a Cistercian monastery in Essex, and William of Newburgh (c. 1136 – c. 1198), an Augustinian canon and historian from Yorkshire. Both men wrote in the late 12th and early 13th centuries, placing the events during the reign of either King Stephen (1135-1154) or King Henry II (1154-1189). While their accounts differ in minor details, they concur on the core elements: the appearance of two green-skinned children, a boy and a girl, speaking an unknown language, wearing strange clothes, emerging from ancient pits near Woolpit in Suffolk, and initially consuming only raw beans. This relatively close historical documentation sets the Woolpit story apart from many purely folkloric tales.

To understand the impact of such an event, one must consider the medieval worldview. The 12th century was a time of strong religious faith, but also a period where belief in marvels, portents, and the existence of strange races of men in distant lands (or even hidden within one's own) was widespread. The natural world was often seen as imbued with supernatural significance, and the boundaries between the mundane and the miraculous were more permeable than in our modern, secular age. The appearance of children with such an unnatural hue and incomprehensible speech would have been deeply unsettling, readily inviting interpretations ranging from the demonic to the divinely enigmatic or the fey.

Over the centuries, numerous theories have been proposed to explain the Green Children. Rational explanations often focus on their peculiar skin colour. One prominent theory suggests they suffered from hypochromic anaemia, then known as "green sickness" or chlorosis, resulting from severe malnutrition. This condition, more common in young women, could impart a greenish tinge to the skin, which might have faded as their diet improved in Woolpit.

Another oft-cited mundane explanation posits that the children were lost or orphaned Flemish immigrants. There was a notable Flemish presence in East Anglia during the 12th century, with communities of weavers and other artisans. Persecution of these immigrants under King Stephen or Henry II could have led to children fleeing and becoming lost, perhaps hiding in woodland or disused pits. Their "strange clothes" and "unknown language" would then be Flemish attire and speech, unfamiliar to the Suffolk villagers. Their greenness in this scenario is sometimes speculatively attributed to arsenic poisoning (perhaps from working with wool dyes, though this is highly conjectural and less likely to result in a healthy green) or again, malnutrition from their ordeal.

More fantastical interpretations link the children to the rich tapestry of British and European folklore. The colour green has long been associated with fairies, elves, and other denizens of the "Otherworld." The emergence of the children from the "wolf pits" – literally holes in the earth – could be seen as a symbolic emergence from a subterranean fairy realm or an underworld. Their initial refusal of all food but green beans might also carry folkloric significance, as specific diets are often attributed to otherworldly beings.

The girl's own account of their origin, "St. Martin's Land," further deepens the mystery. She described it as a subterranean Christian land of perpetual green twilight, separated by a great river from a "land of light." While some have tried to identify St. Martin's Land with known locations or allegorical places, its description remains unique and evocative. St. Martin of Tours was a popular saint in the medieval period, and his feast day, Martinmas (November 11th), was associated with the end of the agricultural year and the slaughter of livestock for winter – perhaps a tenuous link to a harvest-time appearance. The bells they supposedly followed into a cavern could be interpreted as the lure of fairy music or a more mundane sound leading them astray.

The wolf pits themselves are significant. As man-made excavations designed to trap dangerous predators, they represent a liminal space, a boundary between the cultivated human world and the wild, untamed unknown. For the children to emerge from such a place adds to their aura of otherness, as if stepping directly from a symbolic underworld into the human realm.

The enduring appeal of the Green Children of Woolpit lies in this very ambiguity. The story hovers tantalizingly between historical possibility and folkloric marvel. It speaks to our fascination with the "other," with lost worlds, and with the unexplained. The detailed yet ultimately enigmatic accounts of the medieval chroniclers provide just enough fact to make us question, and just enough wonder to allow the imagination to roam free. Whether they were malnourished human children lost in traumatic circumstances, or something far stranger, their story remains a unique and haunting echo from the medieval past, a testament to a time when the world still held a profound capacity for the utterly unexpected.

Epilogue

It is time to gently close the cover on this first volume of "Urban Legends from the UK: Chilling Tales from British Towns and Countryside." We have journeyed together through shadowed lanes and into the heart of ancient manors, stood vigil by mist-shrouded lochs, and listened to the inexplicable whispers within ordinary suburban homes.

From the leaping terror of Victorian London to the spectral hound of East Anglia, from the sorrowful phantom on a lonely Kentish road to the unquiet relic in a Dorset manor, each tale has offered us a glimpse into the hidden narratives that coil beneath the surface of the British Isles. We have pondered the enigma of green-skinned children emerging from the earth, felt the oppressive dread of a modern poltergeist, shivered at the thought of an undead nobleman in a Highgate cemetery, and questioned what truly roams the wild moors or sleeps in the abyssal depths.

These stories, as you have seen, are far more than simple fictions designed to pass a dark evening. They are the cultural breath of the places that birthed them, potent reflections of our deepest human anxieties, our enduring fascination with the inexplicable, and our complex relationship with history, landscape, and the very nature of belief itself. They are the echoes of unexplained events, the personification of local fears, and sometimes, perhaps, the lingering whispers of genuine, unsolved mysteries.

The United Kingdom, a land layered with millennia of human experience, is a fertile ground for such legends. Every ancient stone, every darkened copse, every centuries-old dwelling holds the potential for a story, a memory that refuses to fade. The tales you have read herein are but a selection, a mere dipping of our toes into the vast, often turbulent, waters of British folklore.

As you step away from these pages, perhaps you will find yourself looking at the familiar landscapes around you with new eyes. You might listen more intently to the tales shared in hushed tones in your own communities, or feel a fresh shiver when confronted with a place that seems to hold its breath, heavy with unspoken secrets. For the true power of these legends lies not just in the reading, but in the understanding that the veil between our world and the world of these stories can, at times, feel remarkably thin.

New tales are always being woven, even as the old ones adapt and endure. The human need to narrate the unknown, to give form to our fears and wonders, is as timeless as the landscapes themselves.

So, until we next venture into the shadows together, keep a candle lit against the encroaching dark, but do not be afraid to listen to the sounds it carries. For in every town, in every quiet corner of the countryside, the whispers persist. And some stories, as you now know, never truly end.

Travel safely, and may your own path be free of unquiet spirits – unless, of course, you are seeking them.

F.T. Weaver

THE END

Dear Reader,

Thank you for venturing with me into the unsettling landscapes of these modern urban legends. It is a compelling, if sometimes disquieting, privilege to explore these contemporary myths that mirror our anxieties and the persistent mysteries of our time.

If this collection has resonated with you, perhaps sending a shiver down your spine or sparking a new curiosity about the shadows, please consider leaving a thoughtful review, ideally a 5-star rating, on the platform where you acquired this volume. Your feedback is immensely important: it serves as a signal to other seekers of the uncanny, guiding them toward these stories, and it directly supports my ongoing efforts to investigate and chronicle more of these persistent, resonant legends.

With sincere appreciation for your willingness to explore the darker side of folklore,

F.T. Weaver

Dare to Look Deeper?

The stories you've just read are echoes in the shadowy corners of our modern world. But the whispers never truly fade; new legends form, and old ones resurface with chilling relevance. The journey into the unsettling and the unexplained doesn't have to end here.

If you wish to stay connected to the ongoing exploration of these modern myths and be among the first to learn of new findings and future volumes in this Urban Legends series, I invite you to join my mailing list.

You will receive:

Direct Updates: Be notified when new books in the F.T. Weaver Urban Legends series are released or when there are significant announcements regarding my work in this field.

A Link to the Unseen: Become part of a quiet network of readers who share a fascination with the tales that lurk just beneath the surface of the ordinary.

No barrage of emails, no frivolous extras – just a direct line to further explorations of the legends that shape and haunt our world.

To subscribe, scan the QR code below with your mobile device, or visit https://mailchi.mp/a20199ef4d51/ft-urban-legends.

Keep questioning. Keep listening to the shadows. The legends are always evolving.

F.T. Weaver

Folk Tales
from
Norway

Folk Tales
from
Ireland

Folk Tales
from
Scotland

Folk Tales
from
Japan

Folk Tales
from
Mexico

Folk Tales
from Italy

Folk Tales
from
Nigeria

Folk Tales
from
Germany

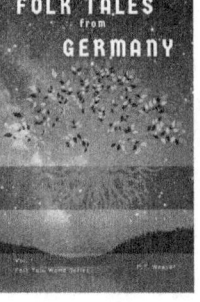

 Folk Tales from India

 Folk Tales from Indonesia

 Folk Tales from Iran

 Folk Tales from France

 Folk Tales from Egypt

 Folk Tales from Brazil

 Folk Tales from China

 Folk Tales from Korea

Folk Tales from Romania

Folk Tales from Turkey

Folk Tales from Canada

Folk Tales from South Africa

Folk Tales from Sweden

Folk Tales from Greece

Folk Tales from Poland

Folk Tales from USA

Printed in Dunstable, United Kingdom